UNSAFE HANDS

Recent Titles by Jane Aiken Hodge from Severn House

BRIDE OF DREAMS

UNSAFE HANDS

Jane Aiken Hodge

SEVERN
SH
HOUSE

This first world edition published in Great Britain 1997 by
SEVERN HOUSE PUBLISHERS LTD of
9–15 High Street, Sutton, Surrey SM1 1DF.
This title first edition published in the USA 1997 by
SEVERN HOUSE PUBLISHERS INC., of
595 Madison Avenue, New York, NY 10022.

British Library Cataloguing in Publication Data

Hodge, Jane Aiken, 1917-
    Unsafe Hands
    1. Detective and mystery stories
    1. Title
    823.9'14 [F]

    ISBN 0-7278-5251-5

Typeset by Palimpsest Book Production Limited,
Polmont, Stirlingshire, Scotland.
Printed and bound in Great Britain by
Creative Print and Design Ltd, Ebbw Vale, Wales.

Author's Note

I wrote this light-hearted whodunnit many years ago when I was just married and living deep in Essex. It is now a period piece and I have hardly touched it.

JAH, 1997

Chapter One

The day was hot. "Remarkable for September," said Mrs Cunningham. "But then we always do have good luck for our flower shows." Her children, wise from experience, suppressed memories of damp bran tubs and sodden coconut shies and agreed.

Anyway, there was no doubt about the heat. Already, at eleven, the long lawn that stretched down to the park fence had a summertime litter of deckchairs and cushions, dangerously enticing to the workers in the field. The house stood wide open to the garden; even the study, normally sacred to Mr Cunningham (and the only place that was) exposed itself with yawning french windows. Inside, Mr Cunningham was revealed doing nothing, as usual, at his desk. If he had done little else in a negative lifetime, he had managed to establish the fact that when it came to the flower show he was useless. "Such a blessing," said Mrs Cunningham, "that I have you dear children to help me now."

Looking back over the years when she had been alone in her dragooning of her parish ladies, she chose to ignore the fact that it was a blessing she had obtained by considerable exertion of force. Her dear children: Penelope, 23, and Gerald, almost 21; knew the flower shows of old and had done their best to escape, but their mother had won, as indeed, she usually did. "But it's always worth trying," Penelope had said as she threw in her hand. Unlike Gerald,

1

she knew how to yield gracefully and so save something from her disasters. This time she had successfully held out for the moral support of a friend.

Now, subsided for a moment in a too-inviting deckchair, she wondered if it had been a good idea. She knew so little about Patience Smith. It was always a desperate business asking one's college friends home; there was too much to explain – and to explain away – in too many directions. Usually though, one did at least know who was on whose side, but not this time . . . What had possessed her to ask Patience, of all people, the acknowledged unknown quantity of her year, the silent sitter-by at other people's fires and other people's parties.

And, final madness, she had forgotten (or been afraid?) to warn her about the flower show, not to mention the birthday. Suppose she hated it and retired, publicly, into one of her silences. Worse still, suppose she was too efficient, suppose she bossed Mother. She was capable of anything, that was certain. But it was too late to worry about it now. A ghost of a whistle and trail of smoke over the far wood announced, as she looked up, that Patience's train was on its circuitous way. "She'll be here in ten minutes and Mother's not even dressed," wailed Penelope.

"Never mind," her brother had just come out of the garden door with an armful of croquet mallets. "She may have missed the train."

"Patience?" Penelope snorted. "She couldn't if she tried. I've never even known her late for a lecture."

"It isn't human . . . d'you know where Mother wants the magic croquet this year?" He put down the mallets in a spillikin heap on the lawn.

"But that's the trouble; she's not – human, I mean. Lord, no, I've no idea – behind the wood, I expect; that's where it was last year."

2

"But *everything's going to be quite different*," the parody of his mother's emphatic delivery dwindled to silence as she appeared round the corner of the house.

"What, my right hands idling the time away!" She bore down on them, formidable in a crimson satin housecoat.

"Yes, Mother, both of them," but Penelope rose. "I was waiting for Patience . . . her taxi's about due."

"Taxis, indeed; a nice ten minute walk . . ."

"Twenty," breathed Gerald.

"Mrs Cunningham; the very person. Could you save our lives with a little string?" A tall, white-haired figure was leaning over the field gate, his look of vague benignity marking him as the vicar no less plainly than his collar.

"You're wanted on the phone, ma'am; Major Balfour." The parlourmaid ('general' on weekdays) succeeded in the interpolation.

"Oh dear, Uncle James; so inconsiderate . . . string? Why, yes, Mr Giles, in the study; I'm sure Mr Cunningham has some . . . but of course, behind the wood, dear boy, we *always* have the magic croquet there. Penelope, here's your friend and I told Mrs Hitchcock the two of you would be there to help with the stall at twelve. Albert, my dear, give Mr Giles the ball of – oh dear, he's disappeared; some people have a genius . . . Mr Giles, be a dear man and find it yourself; it's on the desk somewhere. Yes, Andrews, I'm coming." She talked herself in at the garden door as the local taxi suddered to a standstill at the side of the house.

Patience Smith's air of elegance was deceptive. Her irreproachable tweeds, her bag that matched shoes with exactly the right heel, made Gerald dismiss her at once as useless for the day's purposes. That smooth head would never see the inside of a sack and those precisely nyloned legs could hardly be expected to risk themselves on step ladders or even to negotiate the rougher parts of the field.

3

He rapidly revised his opinion, however, as he watched the calm way she took command of his sister. "You didn't tell me you'd got a party on." Cool grey eyes passed over Gerald to the lawn and across it to the field with its mushrooming tents.

"It's only a flower show." The apology sounded ridiculous.

"So I see. Where do we begin?"

"By taking you up to your room, I should think."

"Oh, don't bother; can't we just dump this somewhere?"

Failing to take the suitcase from her, Penelope led her to the open study windows, where the vicar met them. "Found it at last!" He held up a ball of string in mock triumph, then hurried back to the field.

"I'm so glad . . . oh, here's Father." Penelope introduced Patience, praying to be spared one of her father's odder remarks.

"Delighted you could come," he looked vaguely above her head. "Penelope, who's been messing about in my papers?" He glared at the confused piles on his desk.

"I don't know how you tell, but Mr Giles was just in looking for some string."

"String? Ridiculous; always keep it on the bookcase. Giles ought to know that by now. Probably reading my mail. But he's welcome to what he can find on the desk. I've got more sense than to keep it there, eh Pen?"

His wife's voice in the hall cut him short. "Penelope, Penelope; it's twelve o'clock. Where is that girl?"

For the next three hours, chaos reigned. Doing nothing herself, Mrs Cunningham directed, misdirected and redirected her helpers to just this side of insanity. Exhibits were mislaid, stalls were shifted, tempers lost; a barrel of ice cream melted in the sun; the greasy pig escaped and was caught by Gerald eating prize chrysanthemums in the

4

flower tent. Later, Gerald himself was caught redhanded by his mother as he sneaked behind the flower tent to the path that led to the village. "Where are you off to, Gerald?" She bore down on him, Patience and Penelope in tow.

"I just thought I'd nip over to the village for a sec. Lots of errands to do." He was unspecific.

"Yes, I know those errands. In the Three Feathers, every one of them. You're a disgrace to the Hoblongs, Gerald; and on my great day, too." She wavered between the domineering and the lachrymose.

"But they close in ten minutes and I promised Pennyfold." He knew it was a mistake as soon as he had spoken.

"Pennyfold, indeed. A kitchen hanger-on – and you hobnob with him at the village inn."

"A hobnobbery of Hoblongs," Gerald could not resist it. Then while she was still drawing angry breath: "I won't be ten minutes, I promise. And I really did tell Mrs Hitchcock I'd pick up the tea and sugar for her."

"Oh, very well. I suppose if you must desert me, you must. But who's to write the place cards for me? Penelope's writing's nothing but spider tracks."

"I always print," said Patience. "Would that be any use? It's quite clear . . ."

Gerald gave her a grateful and admiring look. After two arduous hours of grovelling under stalls and balancing on step ladders she looked, miraculously, as neat as when she had stepped out of the taxi. Her hair still shone, her white blouse was still white, her hands – it was impossible – were clean and her nylons unladdered; all this in violent contrast to Penelope whose smudged forehead, untidy hair and begrimed hands bore the marks of all she had done. Even her mother, usually oblivious to anything inconvenient, was compelled to notice her at last. "Penelope, you're a fright. Run home and change at once. You'll miss the opening, but

5

it can't be helped. I don't know how you can get yourself into such a state." She looked complacently down at her unruffled silk dress and pointed scarlet nails.

"Well, thank God for an excuse to miss the opening," said Penelope, as the two girls turned in at the field gate. "Hullo, Uncle James, you'd better hurry; even Father's just arrived and they were all 'after you-ing' on to the platform when we came away. An opening wouldn't be official without you there."

"I know, deplorable. That car of mine wouldn't start again and I had to walk across. I'd never have thought I could have done it the time – I'm puffing like a grampus." He demonstrated. "Not getting any younger I'm afraid. But it wouldn't do to miss the opening. I looked in at the Hall and didn't see a soul so I came straight on – knew I must be pretty late if Albert had gone."

A 'man of distinction', Patience thought, not forgetting the quotation marks. "Major or Colonel?" she asked, as they walked across the lawn.

"Oh, Major," said Penelope. "Good Lord, I never introduced you, I'm so sorry; but he was in such a rush, poor old dear. That's Major Balfour; he lives in that big white house across the railway line," she pointed. "He and Mother were practically brought up together; that's why we call him Uncle James; he's no relation really but he's nicer than most. Your bag's in the study, isn't it? We'll go in that way." But at the study window she paused, "Aunt Fan! I thought you were in bed."

"I heard something, Penny dear. It might have been burglars or it might have been sweet Robin . . . he was all my joy, you know." A tall woman advanced towards them from the dark interior of the study; her long white dress, style of 1920, trailing dimly behind her, her hands full of dark leaves. "These are for his bier." She held them out to Penelope.

6

"But Aunt Fan, you promised you'd stay in bed today; you know you don't feel well." Penelope looked with desperate entreaty at Patience.

"Yes, dear, I know, but we must deck it first." She laid a leafy branch on the back of the study sofa.

"Why don't we do it for you," said Patience, taking the leaves from her other hand. 'I'm very good at biers. You get back to bed and don't worry."

"Well, well, perhaps I will." She wrung her hands. "All the perfumes of Arabia – but I did hear a noise, Penny; it might have been burglars."

"I expect it was Uncle James; he just went over to the show."

"James. Oh – so perfidious. At his head a grass green turf . . . yes, I'll to bed." She trailed away.

Penelope picked up the leaves and replaced them in their vase. "Patience, I am sorry; I meant to warn you, but I thought she was safe out of the way for today at least. She's been like that for ages, poor dear – since she was a girl. She's Mother's sister, you know. Thinks she's all Shakespeare's heroines in turn. It's all right when she's being the comic ones, but it's not so good when she goes tragic. Of course it *would* happen today."

"Ought we to get the doctor?"

"I expect he's at the show; everyone goes. Yes, I expect it would be a good idea; not that there's much anyone can do for the poor dear. She's only a year older than Mother; you wouldn't think it, would you? There was a tragic affair – with Uncle James, believe it or not. Grandpa put his foot down, Uncle James went off and made a fortune; poor Aunt Fan went mad."

"But why?" The girls were changing in Patience's room and the question came from among folds of dark blue silk.

"What? Go mad? Oh, Grandpa, you mean. Well, Uncle

7

James was miles and miles beneath us then. Funny, isn't it? But of course I haven't told you about the Hoblongs."

"The Hoblongs? I thought that was the house: Hoblong's Hall."

"So it is." Penelope was applying lipstick with expert speed. "Shocking mirror this. But it's the family too. Mother and Aunt Fan are the last of the Hoblongs. Sad, isn't it?"

"Is it?"

"Frankly, I couldn't care less. But you should hear Mother. As a matter of fact; I'm afraid you probably will. I meant to warn you that you're in for another family do. This is just a warm-up; it's Gerald's twenty-first birthday on Tuesday."

"Really? I wish you'd told me . . ."

"Oh Lord, don't bother about presents and all that stuff. It's not that . . . Are you ready? Good, Mother'll be champing."

Penelope seemed uneasy as they went downstairs and out again into the dazzling garden. "What a day. Mother's luck, she says. The luck of the Hoblongs, blast them."

"Why blast them?"

"Oh, I feel such a fool." Penelope shut the field gate with a bang and they plunged at once into the noise and confusion of the show, which was in full swing already. The local band was playing an unrecognisable march; children screamed with joy and their parents screamed at them to be quiet; the vicar tried in vain to make himself heard through an inadequate megaphone as he organised the under-fifteen obstacle race. Penelope ignored it all. "The thing is," she went on, "Mother will act as if we were a family with a curse like in Walter Scott. It wouldn't be so bad if we were." Patience laughed. "Well, you know what I mean; if there were a tradition or something, but it's just Mother's nonsense."

An elderly, fattish man with black hair too shiny on a

round head had been trying to catch her attention through the last sentence. "At last," he began floridly, but Penelope interrupted him:

"Oh, good afternoon, Dr Hoblong. I was wondering if I'd see you. I wonder if you'd mind going over and having a look at Aunt Fan; she's a bit queerer today."

"But with the greatest of pleasure, my dear Penelope; your wishes, as always, are my commands." His manner, Patience thought, was almost too bedside to be decent in the hot light of day. But he had turned to her. "A beautiful day for our little show, Miss er . . . you are enjoying it, I trust. But you must be; whatever Mrs Cunningham touches turns to gold."

"Miss Smith, Dr Hoblong," put in Penelope ungraciously; she had half turned away and was paying ostentatious attention to the little boys at the coconut shy.

"Miss Smith," he beamed. "I trust we shall have the pleasure of your company for The Birthday?" The capitals were unmistakable.

"Miss Smith is staying a week." It came from over Penelope's shoulder.

"Happy Miss Smith," he purred. "But I must tear myself away; duty calls, you know. Can I bring you anything from the house, Penelope? A jacket perhaps?" His eyes glanced over her sleeveless shoulders.

But she had turned away. Patience followed her, wondering at her unusual rudeness. "I thought your mother was the last of the Hoblongs?" she hazarded as they paused in the shade of the flower tent to watch the crowd at its entrance.

"So she is." Penelope rose. "Dr Hoblong changed his name. His mother was Mother's aunt; she married a Mr Smith. Oh, I am sorry."

Patience laughed. "That's all right; I haven't changed my

9

name. But what's the matter with the poor man? He seems harmless enough."

"Oh, there's nothing the matter with him." Surprising bitterness charged Penelope's voice. "Only Mother wants me to marry him – for the name, you know. Come on, let's go and do our duty by the flowers and vegetables."

"How does he feel about it?" They were wedged in the crowd beside a wilting table arrangement of belated scabious and old man's beard.

"Couldn't you see? He's an old boyfriend of Mother's and I suppose she wants to keep him in the family. He grovels when she speaks to him. He makes me sick. Your scabious are beautiful, Mrs Pennyfold."

"Thank you, miss; glad you like them, miss." The red-faced woman looked as if only the crowd prevented her from curtsying. "Oh miss," she went on, "it's no time to be troubling you, I know, but if you'd just put in a word for my Jim with your pa and the Major I'd be that grateful. He don't mean no harm, miss."

"I'm sure he doesn't, Mrs Pennyfold; but poaching is poaching, you know." To Patience's amusement, Penelope was suddenly the daughter of the manor. "And tell him he'd better keep away from our kitchen for a bit; Father's really angry this time."

"I will miss, and thank you kindly. You know Jim; he wouldn't hurt a fly." She half-curtsied again.

"He's hurt plenty of our pheasants," said Penelope as she turned away. "Oh, come on, Patience, let's get out of here; it's too hot to breathe," she made a dash for the door, ignoring a row of giant vegetable marrows and some portentous cabbages.

"It's a very feudal part of the world, isn't it?" said Patience as they breathed again in the comparative cool and quietness of the children's exhibit.

10

"You mean all the bowing and scraping? Yes, it gets me down. I'm sure it's what did for Mother; to hear her you'd think the Hoblongs were God. Just because we've lived here for 2,000 years or so. There was a Hoblong at the Battle of Maldon, you know. Or rather Mother knows. He got killed, she says, and serve him right. Some of the kids' drawings aren't a bit bad, are they? I like the murder scene over there."

"It's not a murder; it's an elopement. But do tell me about this birthday business."

"Oh that. It's nothing to do with the family history, if that's what you mean . . . it's just that there's some absurd old document Mother's brother left to be given to Gerald when he's 21. He died in Africa, you know – the hero of the house of Hoblong – years ago, the year Gerald was born."

"But what's in the document?"

"Nobody knows. That part really is rather romantic. When he knew he was dying he sealed it up with his signet ring and threw the ring into the lake . . . I don't remember its name; but one of the big ones. It had gone down from father to son since about Doomsday – the ring I mean – Mother was furious when she heard. Father says it was the thing that pulled her together when she heard Uncle Gerald was dead. She was so angry . . ."

"But what happened to the document?" they had subsided at a tea table and Patience spoke through stale cake.

"Father's got it in his study. Mother said it was too precious to put in a bank – just like her – so Father keeps it in the secret cupboard in the panelling."

"Gracious, how exciting."

"Well, it isn't really; everyone knows where it is. Gerry and I found it when we were little and we had it open so much that now you can see the crack."

"But no one's seen the document?"

11

"Only the outside of it . . . it's a piece of leather, actually, with this damn great seal all over it; you couldn't possibly get it open without breaking the wax. So Gerry opens it on Tuesday after dinner with fanfare of trumpets and it turns out to be an unpaid African laundry bill. It would serve Mother right. D'you want any more tea? All right, let's go. I want to see them chase the greasy pig."

Patience had resigned herself by now to the suddenness with which Penelope dragged her from exhibit to exhibit. It was almost, she thought, as if she were looking for someone. Though really it seemed as if they had seen everyone in Suffolk; she had long since given up trying to keep track of the introductions she had suffered, each with its quota of inanities about the beauty of the day and the more than ordinary success of the show. There had also been constant encounters with Mrs Cunningham, who kept, Patience noticed, a pretty close eye on her children. On his rather red-faced return from the village, Gerald had been forced into service at the shooting gallery, and Penelope, though released from active duty by the presence of her guest, was kept well up to the mark. "Have you bought your ticket for the lucky dip, Penny dear?", "I do hope you girls have been round the children's exhibit; it does encourage the poor little things so" "I didn't see you at the obstacle race, Penelope my lamb?" The remarks pursued them, turning even their visit to the greasy pig into a duty call.

It was a very active little pig and they had seen two young men and a girl in red slacks retire discomfited when Patience felt her companion stiffen. A very tall, fair young man had stepped purposefully into the ring. "Oh God," muttered Penelope, "keep Mother away."

The young man rolled up his shirtsleeves and looked at the

pig. The pig looked back at the young man and sidestepped greasily.

"Friend of yours?" asked Patience.

"Yes and no." Penelope was watching with an odd desperation. A few preliminary passes; then the young man caught the pig by the tail and there was an excited mutter from the crowd, which was clearly very much on his side. But the pig was too quick for him and he was left with a couple of hairs. He held them up for inspection with rueful triumph, while the crowd muttered sympathetically. As the contest progressed it was obvious that he and the pig were a pair of natural comedians with a very proper respect for each other. They were dancing a fantastic minuet round the enclosure and the crowd was in ecstasies when the referee shouted, "Half a minute to go!"

The young man caught Penelope's eye over the crowd. With a farewell gesture worthy of a crusader's last moments he threw himself on the pig. There was a volley of squeals, a suppressed curse or two, a roar from the crowd and it was fairly caught.

"Very unorthodox," said the referee handing the young man a bag for the pig. "But you deserve it." The crowd clearly agreed with him and nobody consulted the pig.

Patience was not surprised to see the young man working his way towards them, pig, poke and all. "Hullo, Pen," he said. "How are you? Haven't seen you for ages. May I lay my spoils at your feet?"

"Peter, how could you . . . oh, this is my friend Patience Smith – Peter Everett."

"How d'you do," he said. "How could I indeed? Natural genius, of course; but I'm glad you're properly impressed."

"Oh, you're hopeless," she wailed, and then again, "how could you?"

He stood there, laughing, triumphant, his face and shirt-front covered with black streaks of grease, the pig whimpering slightly in its bag. "Lord, it's good to see you, Pen; even looking so worried."

"Good afternoon, Mr Everett," Mrs Cunningham's voice fell like an icicle among them. "I'm glad to see you are amusing yourself as usual. Perhaps you would like to go over to the Hall and wash your—" she hesitated, "—hands. You might not want to go home in that state."

"Thanks a lot, Mrs Cunningham. Good of you to let me cross the forbidden threshold. And perhaps I could leave this somewhere." He held up the bag. "I was rather hoping to give it to Pen. Lots of bacon on him."

His cheerfulness in face of Mrs Cunningham's thunderous chill seemed to Patience as gallant as a skiff's musket confronting the Armada. But Mrs Cunningham was not to be thawed. "I am afraid Penelope would have little use for a live pig," she said. Then, "Penny, my dear, come along and talk to Lady Thistlethwaite, she was asking after you. You know your way, Mr Everett." She swept Patience and Penelope away in a silence that was only less oppressive than the things the crowd prevented her from saying. For the rest of the afternoon the two girls were kept strictly in tow and Patience heaved a sigh of relief when she finally announced that it was time to go home.

The crowd had long since hesitated, drifted away from the sideshows, offered itself a last drink at the refreshment tent, accepted it, and vanished. Now only the flagging group of helpers remained, gloomily counting takings or drooping exhaustedly at tent doors and saying what a wonderful show it had been. Mrs Cunningham gathered them together with the practised eye of a hostess and delivered a brief harangue about the privileges of tidying up, with special reference to the park grass. She herself, she explained, was unfortunately

14

prevented from making one of their happy band by the news that her poor dear sister was worse. There were sympathetic murmurs and a few hurriedly suppressed exclamations of relief from the helpers, as Mrs Cunningham and the two girls turned towards the Hall.

Evening was falling; the air was cool at last and birds, inaudible all afternoon, sang in the trees. At the bottom of the far meadow, a toy train wreathed its smoky way into the woods.

"I think I shall go and lie down for half an hour before dinner," said Mrs Cunningham. "It's been a very trying day." The words were spoken directly at Penelope. "Very trying." She drooped away, honourable exhaustion written in every limb.

Gerald was lying full length in a deckchair on the lawn. "I thought you were never coming home," he said. "Peter Everett was here."

"I know. Did you see him?" Penelope brightened perceptibly.

"Of course, I did, silly. He sent you his love. He's going to raise the pig for you. It's to be called Ulysses."

"Ridiculous." But Penelope was near tears.

"There's some sherry in the study. Father's upstairs," Gerald said.

"Sometimes I almost like you, Gerald. Come on Patience. Sherry."

She was still close to tears, Patience noticed, as she poured their sherry into the heavy glasses that stood on a side table in the study. Searching for a neutral subject, Patience remember The Birthday. "Where did you say the famous document was kept?" she asked.

"Oh that. Here's to you." They drank. "Over here. Secret cupboards are always over fireplaces aren't they? So the concealed Jesuit'll keep warm I suppose. You see, there's

15

no deception; you press this panel here, and that boss there, and out she comes." She paused. "That's funny." She reached an arm into the dark gap in the panelling.

Not much room for a Jesuit there, thought Patience. "What's funny?" she asked.

"The document's not there. I suppose Father's cleaning it up a bit ready for the day. It was covered with dust last time I looked. I hate spiders. Oh well," she shut the hidden door. "Sorry about that; you'll have to wait and be properly surprised on Tuesday. Oh, don't say I showed you the cupboard, will you? Mother likes to think it's a deadly secret." She picked up the decanter. "Have some more, this is doing me good. Well, here's to crime."

* * *

Sunday was somnolent. Mr Cunningham had a heavy cold and spent the day over cups of tea in his study. Major Balfour came to lunch but even his presence failed to enliven a dispirited meal. He missed his host, Patience thought, noticing an occasional glance at the door of the study where Mr Cunningham was incommunicado. "I won't have the children catching it," said Mrs Cunningham. "Nursing one is bad enough, but I'm not going to nurse the whole family."

Worn out by the labour of making Andrews take trays into the study, she retired to her room as soon as the Major left and did not reappear till it was time to eat the dismal meal of cold pieces that adds the final touch of respectability to an English Sunday.

Gerald was absent from this feast, having disappeared at seven with a glance at his watch and a muttered apology about an 'appointment'.

"I hope he's not going rabbiting with Pennyfold," said Penelope. "How about some piquet?"

* * *

16

Crisis broke on them early on Monday morning. Not, Patience thought afterwards, that it had seemed like crisis at the time. She and Penelope had been helping the parlour-maid, now in her more usual capacity of 'general', with the dishes. Mrs Cunningham had drifted in. "Can I trust you to do the flowers properly, Penelope? Uncle James is going to drive me into Muchton. Yes dear, we're out here, what's the matter?"

"Oh, there you are." Mr Cunningham looked flurried. "Could I speak to you for a minute?"

"Of course." With a speaking glance at Andrews she joined him in the hall. A minute later she was back. "Penelope, come here a minute, would you?"

Patience went on drying sherry glasses; they were cut glass and took a lot of polishing. "Lovely show Saturday," said Andrews, "I didn't half enjoy myself. Miss Penelope's boyfriend got the greasy pig, I hear." Over her voice Patience heard Mrs Cunningham's voice calling, "Gerald, Gerald; where is that boy?"

The door bell rang. "That'll be the Major." Andrews dried her hands on her apron. "Don't like to be kept waiting, that one. Should have heard him Saturday afternoon; changing for the show, I was, and never heard the bell." Patience went on drying glasses.

"Oh boy, what a do!" Andrews rejoined her all agog. "Haven't seen the Master so put out since he found Jim Pennyfold in my kitchen." She giggled then paused, courting enquiry.

Guest's reticence battled briefly with curiosity and lost. "What's the matter?" asked Patience.

"Coo, matter . . ." It was too good to hurry over. "Master's lost that precious paper he fusses over so. Missed it last night he did and hasn't had a wink of sleep by the look of him. He's turned the study upside down, as if it would walk out of that secret cupboard of his – *secret*!" she sniffed. "Looking under the carpets and everywhere and casting in – in," she gave it up. "Wanted to make out I took it. Much more of that and I'd have been out of this house pretty quick and not back in a hurry. Good thing I happened to look in to the study Saturday night and saw you and Miss Penelope at the cupboard; everyone knows I went straight home at six so of course I couldn't of took it; not when you and Miss Pen saw it at six, and Master cooped up in the study all day yesterday with that cold."

"But," Patience paused. No need to stir Andrews up again; Penelope must have explained to her parents that the document had already been missing when they looked for it.

"Patience," it was Penelope herself, "thank goodness; there you are. Come here a sec, would you." She urged Patience out to the lawn at the back of the house.

Looking back, Patience could see an agitated little group in the study. Mr Cunningham seemed to be poking about in the upholstery of the chairs, while Mrs Cunningham held forth to Major Balfour and Gerald. Penelope looked back too. "There," she said, "that's far enough. Lord, Patience, this is frightful; you won't let me down, will you? I don't know what I'm going to do. You didn't say anything to Andrews, did you? She told you, of course?"

"Yes. No, I didn't say anything. Why should I?"

"Well you see; oh dear, it's frightful; it's all my fault and I've no idea where to get hold of him. What on earth shall I do? But you won't tell, will you?"

"My good woman; I haven't the foggiest idea what you're talking about. Start at the beginning, would you – and better hurry; it looks to me as if the meeting's breaking up. What mustn't I tell?"

"That it wasn't there, of course."

"But, Pen—"

"Oh, don't you see," Penelope interrupted her. "He must have taken it; Mother was so poisonous Saturday afternoon and when she sent him over here to wash he must just have walked in and pinched it to pay her back. It's just like him; and it'll turn up in some ridiculous place or other, round that blessed pig's neck or something. But he doesn't realise: this is serious. I've never seen Father in such a flap."

"But if Peter Everett took it, how on earth did he find it?"

"That's what's so frightful. I showed him; ages ago, before there was all that fuss and Mother said he couldn't come any more. It's all my fault; I've got to find him. Patience, you hold the fort, say anything; say I've an idea where it is, if you like, but don't say it wasn't there on Saturday night. I'm going to Mrs Hitchcock's to telephone. She likes me and she's deaf as a post. Lord, here they come." Penelope fled.

But it was a false alarm. In the study, Major Balfour had merely opened the french windows to see how the catch worked. "A child could force it, Cunningham; I tell you it was asking for trouble to leave it there. If you were in the study all day yesterday someone must have got in the night before. Nobody heard anything, I suppose?" Confronted with Mr Cunningham's ineffectual searchings and his wife's voluble despair, the Major had automatically taken command. "You, Gerald? Your room's next door, isn't it? Did you hear anything?"

"Not a thing, but that doesn't mean much. It'd take the last trump to wake me."

"Oh, Gerald, can't you be serious?" wailed his mother. "For all you know it's your fortune you've lost. I always said it ought to be kept in the bank. To think that I've given in to you all these years, Albert, and now it ends in this. I shall never get over it; never."

19

"But my dear, you know you wanted it kept in the cupboard . . ." Mr Cunningham began.

"One more word and I shall scream." She demolished him, and turned to Major Balfour. "But if someone broke in, oughtn't we to have the police?"

"Well, it's a bit difficult," said the Major. "I don't quite know what they'd say about being called in to investigate the loss of an unknown document. But of course if you like I'll call up Colonel Forrester – he's the chief constable, you know – and put it to him for you."

"But, surely," said Gerald, "when you say 'unknown document', there must be a copy somewhere, or something to say what it is. Isn't there, Father?"

"That's the devil of it," said Mr Cunningham. "There isn't. At least, not exactly. When your uncle Gerald was dying he wrote me a letter and sealed it up the same way as he did the document – with his signet ring."

"Yes," put in Mrs Cunningham, "a family heirloom that should have come to you, Gerald; and he threw it in the lake. Most inconsiderate, I call it; but then Gerald never did have any family feeling. I remember when poor Fan . . ."

"But the letter." For once her son was not prepared to listen to her monologue. "What was in it? Did you keep it?"

"Not very much, really. Yes, I've got it around somewhere, I think. But all it said was that he was sending this paper thing for you; 'it's not much use now', I remember he said, 'but in twenty years or so it might be worth something to young Gerald, so give it him when he's 21' . . . Or something like that. I don't remember exactly."

"But was that all?" Gerald asked. "He must have said something more about the paper?"

"Oh, yes; there was a lot about how he didn't trust anybody so he was sending the letter and document separately,

20

both done up the same with the signet seal, so I'd know if anyone had tampered with them."

"Funny thing how sick men get delusions towards the end," said Major Balfour. "It'd have saved a lot of trouble if he hadn't been so suspicious, wouldn't it?"

"But was the signet ring really so unique?" asked Gerald.

"Of course it was." Mrs Cunningham bridled. "You remember the rings, James? There were two of them originally. One for the eldest son, one for the eldest daughter. Of course it would have been much better if I'd had it; Fan never could look after things and she lost hers in the river one day when we were boating. You remember, James, it was the last time before the row." If Mrs Cunningham felt any discomfort at referring so blithely to the old tragedy, she concealed it well.

"Nobody did open the document, did they?" asked Balfour.

"Of course not. All the seals were perfect. I do remember a funny thing, though." Mr Cunningham rubbed a dirty hand across his forehead. "Gerald said in his letter that he was going to mix the two up; the letter and the document, I mean, and the way he wrote about it, you'd have thought the letter would have got here first – but it didn't, the document got here quite a bit the first – all covered with seals and 'not to be opened till 19 Sept 1950' all over it. I couldn't make head or tail of it, except of course I knew that was Gerald's birthday so I thought it was probably all right."

"And the letter came along later?" asked Gerald.

"Yes, quite a bit later. Not that it was much help, when it did get here; it was all about how he was arranging to get them both here. There was some white man staying at the camp with him; he didn't say much about him, but he didn't seem to trust him, quite; so he was going to tell him the letter was the document and give it to him (they looked just alike,

21

I told you); and the document he gave to a native boy who was going down to the sea anyway."

"Well, one thing; it looks as if he was right about not trusting the white man if the letter took so long to get here," said Gerald. "What was he taking all the time about?"

"Probably held up travelling," said Major Balfour. "You're forgetting what it's like in Africa, my boy. You don't just walk down to the end of the road and get a bus. And he can't have been opening it, can he, Bert; it arrived all in order, didn't it?"

"Oh, perfectly, yes. Just like the other one."

Mrs Cunningham was getting impatient. "It's all very well," she broke in. "Here you go, talk, talk, talk about what happened twenty years ago and all the time what are you doing about finding the thing? My poor boy." She put her arm around Gerald. "First the government takes everything that ought to be yours in taxes, and now your father goes and loses our last hope. I expect it was the deeds to a diamond mine; Gerald sounded awfully cheerful in his last letters, as if he was on to something. I'm sure that was it; we'd all have been rich and I could have had new slip covers. And then just because your father will insist on keeping the paper in his miserable secret cupboard . . . As if everyone in Muchton didn't know where it was!"

"But my dear, as a matter of fact . . ."

"But, Mother . . ."

"No good crying over spilt milk." The Major's powerful voice drowned the more tentative protests of Cunningham and Gerald. "Though I must say I've often thought I was the only person in the district who didn't know where that cupboard was. Just as glad I didn't, as it's worked out. Ingenious, though," he opened and shut the concealed cupboard door. "But you're quite right, Violet. We must decide what we're going to do. There's no doubt about its being lost, Albert? You've looked everywhere?"

"Of course. When I missed it last night I just thought it had slipped down in the cupboard or something. But it's not there. You can see." A forlorn gesture included the empty cupboard and the ravaged room.

"And we know it was here about six on Saturday when Penelope and her little friend looked at it. Right. Now the question is, were there any strangers in the house Saturday night, or did someone break in after you were in bed? Anyone hear anything?"

"Not a thing." Gerald spoke for them all.

"But of course anyone could have got in by this window pretty well at any time, couldn't they? Were you in here at all Saturday evening, Bert?"

"No. Violet likes . . . I mean I like to sit with the family in the evening."

"Quite, quite. And the drawing-room's on the other side of the house. So they could have got in any time."

"Yes, they *could*," said Gerald. "But how did they know where it was? Nothing else was disturbed, was it, Father?"

"Nothing that I noticed."

"What about the girl?" The Major was in full control. "Did she notice anything when she did the room this morning? Footmarks, perhaps? Mud on the rug? Anything?"

"I don't know. Fetch her, would you, Gerald?" Mr Cunningham's was almost a parody of the Major's outburst of efficiency.

But Andrews, when she appeared, was not helpful. Amid voluble protestations of innocence she maintained that the room had been entirely as usual. Yes, the french windows had been shut. "Mud," she sniffed. "What with the show, and the whole village making this house their barn all day Saturday, there wasn't nothing but mud. By the windows?

23

Course it was by the windows. Who goes round by a door and wipes his feet when he can make a little extra work for someone tracking mud in the window. Why, there was Dr Hoblong and young Mr Everett and—"

"Yes, yes," the Major interrupted her, "we know a lot of people were in on Saturday afternoon, but what we want to know is if someone got in at night."

"Blessed if I know." The crisis was giving Andrews a comfortable feeling of equality with her employers.

But it was not shared. "Thank you, Andrews," said Mrs Cunningham frostily. "That will do."

"Well, that's no use," said Gerald. "No perfect set of the criminal's footprints left obligingly on the axminster. Which remind me; how about fingerprints, Father? Have you looked for them?"

"Gerald, for the thousandth time, will you be serious?" said his mother. "I should have thought you of all people would have realised that this is no laughing matter. For all you know you may have lost a fortune, and I don't know where else you're going to find one. A little bird whispered something to me the other day about college debts and I hope you don't think your father's going to pay them."

"Debts?" Mr Cunningham had been looking anxiously in the cupboard as if he hoped the missing document had rematerialised there; but that word brought him back into the conversation. "I hope it's nothing serious, Gerald?" Gerald reddened, looked at the floor, and said nothing.

"Boys will be boys, I suppose," put in the Major soothingly.

"That's all very well when it's not your boy," said Mr Cunningham. "Now then, Gerald, out with it. How much?"

Gerald was saved by Andrews. "Dr Hoblong, Ma'am," she said and drew aside to let him in.

24

Dr Hoblong's face shone with heat, his hair with brilliantine. "Mrs Cunningham," he panted slightly, "you will pardon this intrusion, I am sure, but I cannot believe . . ." He wiped his brow with his oversize, overbright silk handkerchief and began again. "I felt it my duty." He was pleased with the phrase. "Yes, I really felt it my duty . . ." His large eyes swept the company. "But we are not alone. I must apologise; I was carried away. You know my feelings towards Penelope too well; you will forgive me."

"But what's the matter?" asked Mrs Cunningham. "You're trying to frighten me, Dr Hoblong, but I'm sure Penelope's quite old enough to take care of herself. She certainly cares little enough about anyone else; I suppose she's off with that Patience of hers now, when I particularly need her at home. But of course she's young . . ." She belatedly remembered Hoblong's position as Penelope's favoured suitor.

"Of course," he agreed with her blandly. "But she's not out with Miss Smith, you know. I left her at Mrs Hitchcock's telephoning just five minutes ago." He paused expectantly.

"At Mrs Hitchcock's? Telephoning? What a very extraordinary thing to do. Our telephone's not out of order, is it Albert?"

"No dear, not that I know of."

"Oh, I expect it was nothing." Hoblong was intentionally unconvincing. "Of course dear old Mrs Hitchcock's so fond of Penelope and so very deaf . . ."

"Did you hear who she was talking to?" Mrs Cunningham's was the voice that launched a thousand meetings.

"Well, I did just happen . . . but I hardly like . . . It's not my place to interfere between mother and daughter . . . but I did think she'd been forbidden . . ." He paused, awaiting pressure.

"Don't play with a mother's feelings, Dr Hoblong. Who was it? Surely it cannot have been Peter Everett?"

25

"I might have known I'd never be able to keep anything from you, dear Mrs Cunningham. Against such quickness, such perception, what can I do? Yes, I'm very much afraid it was young Everett, or rather his mother, I believe; but of course I'm sure there is some simple explanation. I happened to be passing Mrs Hitchcock's a short while ago and hearing Penelope's voice I remembered that it was high time I enquired after the poor lady's deafness – growing rapidly worse, I fear; she totally failed to hear me knock."

"Bet you never did," put in Gerald under his breath.

"And I was forced to walk in. And what did I hear but Penelope talking to Mrs Everett on the telephone and begging her to have Peter get in touch with her at once. I didn't know what to do. I'm so devoted to Penelope, but of course I knew that you've so wisely forbidden her see young Everett . . . and finally my sense of duty triumphed and here I am to tell you all – but unwillingly and with a sad heart," he ended nobly.

"And quite right too," said Mrs Cunningham. "I'm shocked at Penelope. Such flagrant double-dealing I have never heard of. Why only last night she promised, yes promised me on her word of honour that she would not speak another word to Peter Everett. I'm shocked, I tell you, shocked and mortified. Catching the greasy pig, indeed. Competing with all the rag-tag and bobtail of Suffolk and then the impertinence to offer his disgusting prize to Penelope. But this shall be the end of it. Doctor Hoblong, I can't tell you how grateful I am to you. I shall remember, I promise you."

"Yes, and so will Pen," said Gerald. But again his comment was unobserved, drowned this time by the Major's powerful voice.

"Mrs Cunningham," he said, "It occurs to me – if you will pardon a mere eavesdropper for making the suggestion –

26

that perhaps there is a little more in this than you realise. Why is Penelope – a good girl usually, one would have said – why is she flatly disobeying your most serious orders? Why? Because she knows Peter Everett has the document and wants to make him give it back before the thing gets any more serious." He listened to their surprised gasps and hurried on. "Mark you, I'm not saying that little Penny had anything to do with it herself; I'm sure she'd never do such a thing, but she might easily know something about it. There's your solution, Albert," he turned triumphantly to Mr Cunningham, "and I hope before the day is over that we'll be congratulating you on the return of the paper. Young Everett's a bit of a troublemaker, but he's no fool; threaten him with the police and you'll have the paper back in ten minutes. And now, if you'll excuse me, I must be off. I've got to catch the Muchton train – business in London this afternoon, I'm afraid; or nothing would drag me away till we'd had young Everett on the carpet and got the whole situation cleared up. But look here, Albert; I'll be back on the seven o'clock. Why don't you walk over for a glass of sherry before dinner and tell me how you've got on and I'll run you back. You don't eat till eight, do you Violet? Good. Seven o'clock sharp, mind. Time and sherry wait for no man – but you're always punctual, Bert; no need to remind you. Suppose you don't want to come into Muchton now, Violet? Gerald? No. Well, I'll be on my way. Good hunting." He paused on the threshold. "Here's young Pen coming up the garden. Don't be too hard on her, Violet. Would you give me a hand with the crank, Bert, she's not running right yet."

"Of course. Your hat's in the hall, isn't it?" They left by the door as Penelope crossed the lawn from the orchard gate.

Dr Hoblong seemed to shrink as Penelope approached. "I won't intrude any longer, Mrs Cunningham," he said.

"Perhaps," he glanced out the window, "perhaps it would be best if you didn't mention how you happened to find out about Penelope. Doing one's duty is sometimes very painful, you know; I only hope any small sacrifice I may have made will be of assistance to you in finding this paper or whatever it is that's missing. But I must go. Duty calls. I'll let myself out this way, if I may." He beat an undignified retreat through the door as Penelope opened the french window.

The good weather had broken in the course of the morning and a gust of wind and fine rain blew in with her. "Phew," she said, "just got in in time. It's going to pour. Where's Patience?"

"Patience, indeed!" In a woman who pretended to less elegance it would have been a snort. "Patience is all you can think of after bringing your mother into humiliation and public disgrace. I don't know what possessed me to have a daughter . . ." she was fairly launched.

"Come on Gerald," Mr Cunningham looked at his furious wife, then at his daughter, "we'd better go round and shut the windows." They left Penelope to her fate.

Patience had stood around for a while, pretending, for the benefit of an imaginary audience, to be admiring the giant red dahlias by the field gate. Relieved that no one had thought to ask her anything about the missing document, she hoped that she might succeed in keeping out of the way of questions until Penelope returned from her telephone call. She was neither a practised nor an enthusiastic liar and felt considerably irritated with Penelope for involving her in such a deception. It was all very well for her to want to protect her friend – but was it? If the document was really important the sooner it was back in safe keeping the better. From what she had seen of Peter Everett anything might

28

happen to it while it was in his pockets. She shrugged her shoulders, it was none of her business; she had tacitly agreed to Penelope's action and now she must stand by her.

She moved irresolutely towards the group of deckchairs but decided that they were too close to the study windows. Best not call attention to herself. She went back to the field gate and leant against it looking across the corner of the orchard to the flower show field in the hope that she would see Penelope returning on the footpath that led to Lesser Muchton. But there was no sign of her and she turned back towards the house. The group in the study looked larger; yes, she could recognise Dr Hoblong's heavy figure. Oily man, she thought, poor Penelope. A drop of rain fell on the back of her hand and she shivered in the chill that precedes a storm. There was hardly time to get round the back of the house to the kitchen door; the garden door, right beside the study windows, was far too visible. As the rain began to fall more heavily she remembered the summer house that stood at the corner of the lawn opposite the field gate.

A neglected folly of Penelope's grandfather's, it was a summer house by Charles Adams, Patience thought, brushing aside a giant cobweb, but the rain was coming down in sheets and she sat gratefully in a down-at-heels garden chair that was placed to command the view across the lawn to the study. Although the octagonal building had small-paned glass windows all round, most of the view was cut off by a thick growth of rhododendrons and it was only possible to see out of the windows that looked out on to the lawn and those that gave across the fence to the field that sloped down towards the railway line. Patience thought with amusement that what must have been, in Jane Austen's time, a very pretty little wilderness where a heroine could keep her feet dry and her romance warm, was now getting dangerously like the genuine article. Planted originally, no doubt, to mask the kitchen end of the house, it now ran rampant from the main road to the picket fence that bounded the garden proper, and from the kitchen and study windows to the river Much, which ran along the south-western side of the garden and down through the woods to the railway line. Penelope had told her that the Much formed the boundary between Major Balfour's land and Mr Cunningham's – and she tried vainly to trace its course through the woods to the railway line. But it was all too thick on that side and she turned instead to look at Major Balfour's square white house on the other side of the valley. A puff of smoke in the woods announced one of the two-carriage trains that shuttled up and down between Greater Muchton and Camchester. "The slowest service in the Eastern Region, and that's saying plenty," as Penelope said. And indeed, as Patience watched and listened she could tell that, true to its reputation, the train was slowing down for the right-of-way crossing of the footpath to Major Balfour's and the short tunnel at the end of the valley. She strained her eyes to see if she could see a single occupant, but it was too far to be sure through the curtain of fine rain. It was getting colder and darker than ever in the summer house and – surprising how few of the window panes were broken – positively stuffy. Or rather, Patience realised, there was a strong and to a non-smoker very unattractive smell of tobacco. She looked down. No wonder. The ground at her feet was littered with ash; she was not the only person who had found the summer house convenient. And very recently too, she thought, judging by the strong smell and long, perfect cylinders of the ash.

Her thoughts were interrupted by the sound of loud voices at the back of the house. Mr Cunningham's suddenly sounded out louder than the rest, "And if I ever find you here again, I'll do it, too." Although so vague the threat sounded sufficiently formidable for Patience to revise her opinion of mild little Mr Cunningham. A mixture of curses and threats answered him, and she heard Andrews' voice raised in intercession. But whatever was going on was clearly none of her business, and, realising that the conference in the study must have broken up while she was watching the train, she decided to make a dash for it. Obviously Penelope would not return till the storm was over and the best thing she could do was head for her room and stay there till lunch. She put her scarf over her head and ran.

Chapter Two

Patience closed the garden door gently behind her. But as she did so, hope vanished. At the same moment the study door opened, revealing Penelope in tears, and Mr Cunningham swung violently through the swing door from the kitchen. "And if it happens again," Mrs Cunningham was perorating behind Penelope, but for once her husband's voice was too strong for her.

"That scoundrel Pennyfold was in the kitchen again. I've told Andrews that if we find him here once more, she goes and we prosecute. And I mean it." An angry snort answered him from the kitchen. "Now then, Pen," he turned to his daughter and his voice became gentler at sight of her drowned face. "What's all this about young Everett taking the paper? Young rascal, but I'm grateful it's no worse. Tell him to have it back this afternoon and we'll say no more about it."

"You'll do no such thing." Mrs Cunningham swept out of the study. "It's a valuable piece of property he's taken and he shall suffer for it. Oh why didn't you have the sense to make James phone Colonel Forrester, when he suggested it? Then the paper would be here by now. But you must get him to call him the very first thing when you get over there tonight; though what James means by asking you by yourself I can't think. I suppose I'm to sit at home and think for the pack of you. I'm sure no one else ever does."

"But, my dear," Mr Cunningham finally managed to get it in. "Surely there's no need to bother Colonel Forrester if young Everett returns the paper this afternoon?"

"This afternoon indeed. And what makes you think he's going to? He's vanished with it. His own mother doesn't know where he is. On his boat, she says. A fine story; I wonder you swallowed it, Penelope."

"But, Mother, you know he's always on that boat. And we don't know he's got the paper. After all lots of other people might have taken it; I just thought it might be him because . . ."

"Because I very properly put him in his place on Saturday afternoon, I suppose. But now, Albert, you see we've got to get the police. Of course the boy's got it, but he may be anywhere between here and the Broads and most likely using bits of it to clean that filthy pipe with. I'd have you ring up Colonel Forrester yourself only you wouldn't do it so well as James, he's fifty times the man you are. And now," she turned to Penelope, "to make up for what you've said about him, you will ring up Dr Hoblong and invite him to lunch."

"Mother, I can't. You know what he'll think if I do."

"And so much the better. You ought to be flattered and proud he takes so much trouble for you after the disgraceful way you've behaved. Now then, there's the phone."

"Father, please . . ." Mr Cunningham's face showed how unusual the appeal was. But for once he rose to it. "I'll ring up Hoblong if you like, my dear. Pen's had a hard morning. And as a matter of fact I think it would be a good idea if he had a look at poor Fan; I don't quite like the looks of her today. I found her trailing about upstairs with that old gun of mine and muttering that she was more an antique Roman than a Dane. I don't know what it was all about, but I didn't like the sound of it. And, you know, I really think we should let Pen make up her own mind about Hoblong; after all, it's her affair." He moved to the telephone and dialled as he spoke. From mild Mr Cunningham it was an ultimatum and there was almost a hush in the room as he lifted the receiver.

Lunch was not a cheerful meal. Delighted to be asked, Dr Hoblong outdid himself in complimentary speeches to Penelope, and, when she refused to listen to him, to her mother. Mr Cunningham was silent and preoccupied, while Gerald, who had arrived five minutes late, obviously from the Three Feathers, did not improve matters by a too loud and cheerful description of the local reaction to the excitements at the Hall. Patience, to whom it was addressed, did her best to tone him down by subdued and monosyllabic replies, but it was no use; Gerald helped himself lavishly to bottled beer and went on with his tale. "And Jim Pennyfold says . . ." his voice drowned that of Hoblong, who had been turning a laboured compliment on Mrs Cunningham's housekeeping. She ignored him and rose to her feet:

"Gerald, this is too much. I do not wish to hear any more about your low companions at my table."

She swept from the room and upstairs to lie down while her husband took the doctor up to see her sister. Curious, Patience thought, how it was taken for granted that Mrs Cunningham had nothing to do with the invalid. "Must spare Mother's poor nerves," said Gerald, answering her thought. "Come on, Pen wants a council of war in the nursery." She followed him up to the shabby room on the third story that was still the young Cunninghams' refuge.

"Did he ask for me?" Penelope looked desperate. She had fled up there before coffee was served.

"No, but he's not gone yet. He's with Aunt Fan now."

"Is Mother with him?"

"Of course not; Father. She's lying down."

34

"That's all right then. Everything's in such a stew I thought he might propose again on the strength of it. Didn't you think there was a nasty proprietory look in his eye at lunch, Patience? But God bless Father, say I. You should have heard him, Gerry. He came down like a ton of bricks."

"He came down pretty hard on Pennyfold, too," Gerald put in his side of the story. "I don't know what's got in to the old man. If it's losing the paper; it's almost worth it. But seriously, Pen, what about it? D'you think there's any chance of getting hold of Peter?"

"Lord, I don't know. It's pretty grim. His mother says he went off first thing in the morning, promised he'd phone her in a day or two, but you know how he is when he gets off – it might be a week or more. She was in a frightful flap last time. Of course I asked her to have him call me right away, but I didn't like to make it sound too urgent. She sounded pretty flabbergasted as it was."

"I don't wonder, with Mother practically reading her the riot act last time. Poor old Pen; it is tough. And all the time he may not have it."

"You know, that's what I keep thinking." She looked at him gratefully. "Because surely, Gerald, you were here when he came over to wash?"

"Well, I was, but I didn't go in and hold his hand while he did."

"No, I suppose not," her face fell.

"No," Patience interposed. "But how big was this document? He was in flannels and a shirt, wasn't he? He couldn't have hidden much."

"Good for you. Nor he could, it's quite a solid bit of work," said Gerald. "But he might have put it somewhere and come back for it. Or he might have come earlier – or later, for the matter of that."

"No, not later," Penelope coloured. "Actually, I saw him get on the five o'clock bus . . . unless he came back much later; but really why should he, Gerry?"

"Why should anyone? I do wish we knew when the wretched thing was last seen. There were such a mass of people in and out of the study that day. You'd better hurry up and come clean about it not being there on Saturday evening, Pen. I bet Father goes off the deep end again."

"Yes, I suppose I must." Penelope hastened to change the subject. "There were plenty of people in and out the day before, too. You remember, it was Mother's bridge Friday."

"Good Lord, so it was. They play in the study and have tea in the drawing-room," he explained to Patience. "I suppose any of the old trouts could have nipped in and pinched the thing while the others were at tea."

"I'm backing Mrs Hitchcock," said Penelope. "She makes a point of knowing too much. And she may be deaf, but she gave me an awfully nasty look when I asked the operator for Mrs Everett this morning; and she would hover round all the time I was talking, too."

"Good Lord," said Gerald. "Mr Giles."

"How d'you mean, Mr Giles?" asked his sister.

"Don't you remember? He came asking for string just before Patience's taxi arrived."

"Goodness, yes. And Father had vanished, and Mother sent him into the study to look for it," put in Penelope.

"Yes, and he took a very long time too. But why on earth should he want my document?"

"Oh dear," said Penelope, "this is where we came in: if we only knew what was in the blessed thing!"

"What about the letter explaining it?" asked Patience. "Mightn't it be a good idea to have a look at that? I mean, it might give some kind of a clue."

36

"Good for you," it was the second time she had earned Gerald's commendation. "Let's go and ask Father. Old Hoblong must be gone by now."

But in the front hall they found Mr Giles who had just been let in by Andrews. "I'm afraid Mr Cunningham's out," she was saying, "but I'll call Mrs Cunningham, if you like."

Mr Giles looked as if he would like nothing less, but he was fairly caught by the arrival of the son and daughter of the house and allowed himself to be led into the drawing-room. "Chance for a spot of cross examination," muttered Gerald to Patience as he held the door for her.

Mr Giles was ill at ease. He had come, he explained, rather gratuitously Patience thought, to see if he could be of any comfort to Miss Hoblong. "I saw Dr Hoblong in the village, and he tells me she's not so well today. I was so sorry to hear it." The conventional phrases rang brittle and unconvincing and he showed little surprise when Penelope explained that her aunt was not well enough to see visitors. The conversation dwindled, died, and then was brutally revived by Gerald:

"I expect you've heard we've lost the family document?" he said.

"Yes, as a matter of fact I did hear something about it. Trying for you, but of course it'll turn up somewhere; things don't just disappear, do they?" ("Not much of a guilty start about him, said Penelope later.) He looked at his watch. "Really, I must be going. I'll look in on Mr Cunningham."

"But you must stay to tea," said Gerald, unusually hospitable. "And besides," he stuck to his point, "it rather looks as if the document *had* just disappeared, and we were wondering if perhaps you could help us."

"I?" Even in astonishment Mr Giles managed to be grammatical.

37

"Yes. You remember: you were in Father's study on Saturday morning; we wondered if you'd noticed anything unusual. It took you rather a long time to find the string, didn't it?" Gerald obviously saw himself as prosecuting counsel in a star trial.

However crude his method, it had its effect. Slowly, unmistakably, agonisingly, Mr Giles blushed. "Oh, oh, I see what you mean. Saturday morning. But surely," he was collecting himself, "surely, I understood; I mean your Andrews told my Mrs Pennyfold that the document was still in its place at six."

"Of course it was." For once in her life Mrs Cunningham had entered a room unnoticed. "Penelope and Patience saw it."

Gerald looked at Penelope. "Fat's in the fire anyway by now, Pen. Better come clean."

It was Penelope's turn to blush. "Actually, Mother, the document wasn't there when Patience and I looked for it."

"So you see," Gerald prevented a tirade from his mother by rapid speech to Mr Giles, "it might have been taken any time that day." Mr Giles, who had been recovering himself, blushed again and Patience was uncomfortably aware of his adam's apple. But Mrs Cunningham swept all before her and saved him from answering.

"But that explains everything," she said. "I must say I had been wondering if even Peter Everett would have stolen it from our house at night; but of course he took it in the afternoon. That'll be a lesson to me against being kind to people. And what you children mean by badgering poor Mr Giles about it when he wants his tea I cannot think. Now, I don't want to hear another word about it until Peter Everett has returned it. Mr Giles, sugar and milk? Children, do you know where your father is? He's very late for tea."

38

"Andrews says he went out somewhere after Dr Hoblong left," said Penelope.

"Well, I think it's very inconsiderate of him not to have left a message; but of course nobody thinks of me. Have another scone, Mr Giles. There's no sense leaving any for Albert; I don't suppose he'll be back for hours."

She was more right than she expected. The conversation dwindled and lagged and still there was no sign of Mr Cunningham. Mr Giles looked at his watch at last. "I'm afraid I'll have to run along, Mrs Cunningham. Our cricket club meeting's at half past six and I've got to get back to the vicarage and collect the papers. I'd hoped to have persuaded Mr Cunningham to walk over with me, but I really don't believe I dare leave it any later. I hope . . . I mean I'm afraid it looks as if he's going to miss the meeting."

"Perhaps he's going straight there," said Gerald, and Patience thought Mr Giles's face fell. "Anyway, I'll walk down with you, if you like. The meeting's at the Feathers isn't it? No, Mother, I won't be late for supper."

Mr Cunningham finally appeared, full of apologies, at a quarter past six. "I'm so sorry, my dear; took longer than I expected; hoped I'd find young Peter for you, Pen," the aside was under cover of a stream of complaints from his wife. "But he wasn't there. Too bad. And now I must change pretty quick if I'm to be over at James's by seven. I don't want to let him down when he says I'm so punctual, do I?" His attempt at cheerfulness rang feebly, Patience thought, looking at his drawn face and the tired lines under his eyes. The loss of the document might be little more than a game to Gerald and Penelope but it was obviously telling on him.

Ten minutes later he looked in again. "I'm off now; James is driving me back, Violet, so I'll be in plenty of time for supper."

"But are you really going to walk across the park?"

39

asked Mrs Cunningham with unusual solicitude. "It's almost dark already and James says the poachers are out around there again."

"Young Pennyfold, I expect; but I'll bother him more than he does me. Good Lord, it's half past six already. I must be off; it's a good half hour's walk in this light, and I don't want to take the field path: too wet. See you soon after eight."

He vanished and quiet settled on the party. Mrs Cunningham went off to change for dinner and the two girls sat by the study fire talking aimlessly; too tired even to play at detectives. Suddenly Penelope looked up. "Did you hear something? Thank goodness." She hurried over to open the front window. "Peter," she let him in, "You've got here!"

"You really sound pleased to see me," he smiled down at her and it seemed to Patience that a wave of warmth and laughter had come in with him. "It's almost worth it," he went on, "however much disgrace I'm in."

"Then you did take it. Oh Peter, how could you?"

"Well, in a manner of speaking I took it. I must say I thought better of you, Pen; I thought you'd find it in five minutes."

"Find it?"

"Of course. You don't think I pinched the thing, do you? Really, what a girl. Now then; three guesses."

"Peter, I'll never speak to you again."

"Oh yes you will. I didn't even take it out of the study, if that makes it any easier for you, halfwit."

"Good Lord, the loose board."

"But of course. Positively no deception, ladies." He went down and took up a section of carpet. "The loose board." He lifted it. "There's your blessed document, and some old stale chocolate of yours, Pen, left over from God knows when." With a mock bow he handed a small package to Penelope and the mouse-nibbled chocolate to Patience. "But I hear your mother's angel step. I must vanish; bless you, Pen, forgive me." He blew her a kiss, swung open the study window and disappeared into the gathering darkness.

"He's going by the shortcut," said Penelope, "I hope he doesn't catch up with Father. How could we have forgotten the loose board! Let's put it back where it belongs before Mother comes in; I can't face it all now."

It was not Mrs Cunningham, but Andrews who looked round the door. "Beg your pardon, I'm sure," she said. "I thought Mrs Cunningham was here; it's about the dessert: there aren't enough eggs."

"Oh dear," said Penelope. "No, she's upstairs changing, I think."

"That she isn't," said Andrews with lugubrious triumph. "I just looked. I can't see her anywhere, nor yet Miss Fan."

"That's very odd; it's not the sort of night for taking a stroll."

"But about the dessert, miss? I can't make a sweet soufflé with two eggs, not nohow."

"Oh, open a tin, Andrews; some peaches out of your hoard. But it's queer for Aunt Fan to be out so late," she went on after Andrews left.

"Do you think we ought to go and look for her?" asked Patience

"Oh, I don't know. I've always thought she was really a lot saner than anyone gave her credit for. Besides, Mother's probably with her." But she went to the french windows, opened them and peered out. "It's getting horrid dark. Hullo, Mother's right, there are poachers about." A shot had sounded dully from towards the railway line. "Perhaps Mother's out stalking them; I wouldn't put it past her. She'd love to catch poor Jim Pennyfold red-handed. I don't know

41

why she's so down on him really. It isn't as if there weren't plenty of rabbits. Perhaps it's because she doesn't want to lose Andrews. He's been after her ever since they were at school, but so far Mother's always persuaded her to say no because he's 'such a wild young man'." Penelope's imitation of her mother's voice was not quite so good as Gerald's. "But I don't know why I'm boring you with all this. How about some piquet before supper?"

"Is there time before we change?" Patience looked doubtfully at the clock, which said seven.

"Oh, Lord yes, there's loads of time; that clock's always fast. Listen, there's the seven o'clock train; it always passes here at quarter to."

They drew their table close to the fire and settled down to their game. It was very quiet in the house. As she shuffled the rather dog-eared cards Penelope's thoughts wandered. Where on earth could Mother and Aunt Fan have got to? She thought of going out to look for them, but hesitated, dreading Gerald's ridicule when he got back. If only Father were at home; he'd do something. Poor Father; he'd stood by her nobly about Dr Hoblong and would suffer for it, she was sure. Anyway, there had been no more shots, so the poachers must have moved away; no chance of Mother or Aunt Fan running into them. But what could they be doing? She spoke up at last. "I wonder if we ought to do something about Mother and Aunt Fan?"

"It does seem awfully late to be out for a walk." Patience nodded. "It's beginning to get really black." She turned towards the door. "There's someone coming now."

"So there is." Penelope opened the door and looked out into the hall. "Oh Mother, it's you. We thought you were changing. Have you seen Aunt Fan?"

"Of course I haven't." Mrs Cunningham spoke crossly, rather taken aback, Patience thought, at being caught coming in. "I've been looking all over for her. I saw her from my window – over by the summer house and going down towards the river and I've been looking for her ever since. Of course none of you children would think of coming and helping."

"You should have come and told us, Mother," Penelope said. "We thought you must be out together. You didn't see her at all?"

"Not a sign. And ruined a good pair of nylons, too. You bright young things had better go and see if you can do any better. I must go and lie down for a while before dinner. My poor head's splitting."

"I hate to drag you out," Penelope got up reluctantly. "She's probably down by the river weaving garlands. She's been Ophelia for days. I think she must bone up on her Shakespeare on the sly. All right, Mother, I'm going. But there's really no reason why you should bother, Patience."

"Of course I'll come."

They were out in the hall putting on some of the assortment of old family rainwear that hung in the cupboard there when the front door opened and Aunt Fan drifted in, a garland of damp leaves in her hair, her long dress soaking and bedraggled.

"Good Lord, Aunt Fan, where have you been?" asked Penelope.

Aunt Fan wrung her hands. "Alas," she said, "my poor fool is dead." She took a few mincing steps down the hall towards them and broke into song, her thin voice surprisingly true:

" 'My shroud of white, stuck all with yew,
Oh, prepare it.
My part of death, no one so true
Did share it.' "

43

She dropped a deep curtsy and changed her tune:

> " *'Those are pearls that were his eyes*
> *Of his bones are corals made . . .'* "

She went on singing as Penelope and Patience coaxed her upstairs to her room. They were persuading her to take off her soaking dress and stockings when they heard the telephone.

"Oh, bother," said Penelope. "I'd better go. Come on, Aunt Fan, into bed with you."

But as she closed Aunt Fan's door, the front door banged open below them and Gerald came in with a blast of fresh air. He went straight across the hall to the telephone and they heard him pick up the receiver. "Hullo," he said. "Oh, yes . . . He hasn't? . . . That's funny. Just a sec, while I find out. I only got in this minute myself." His words came fast and blurred. "Hey, Pen," he called.

"Yes?" Penelope leaned over the bannisters.

"It's Uncle James. He's wondering why Father hasn't turned up. What's going on?"

"Hasn't turned up? But he left here ages ago."

"At half past six," put in Patience. She, too, was hanging over the bannisters.

Gerald picked up the receiver again. His colour was high and his motions were deliberate, Patience thought, as if they cost him a considerable effort of control. "Yes," he said, "he left here sharp at half past; he ought to have got to your place by seven . . . Yes, I suppose something must have delayed him . . . Oh yes, perhaps; we did hear some shots, come to think of it. Perhaps he's caught 'em . . . yes, I am sorry; tiresome for you . . . Excuse me a minute." They heard Mrs Cunningham's voice break in:

"Tell Uncle James dinner's at eight and no nonsense;

44

what can your father be thinking about taking so long to get over there?"

But Gerald was listening to the telephone. "Right," he said at last, "We'll expect you both at eight if we don't hear from you." He rang off. "That's odd," he said, more to Penelope and Patience on the stairs than to his mother at his elbow. "It's not like Father to be late. I hope he's all right."

"Of course he's all right," said Mrs Cunningham. "What on earth could happen to him between here and James's? If you ask me it's a put up thing between them to make a good excuse for being late back. Penelope, it's high time you were changing; there's the half hour striking." Her accusing eye included Patience.

At quarter to eight the telephone rang again, and once more Gerald answered. At the doors of their adjoining rooms, changed but not yet lipsticked, the two girls listened unashamedly.

"He's not there yet?" Gerald's voice had a higher note now. "No, he's not back here . . . Yes, I think we'd better . . . It's very odd . . . Yes, I'll see you at the railway bridge."

"Well?" Mrs Cunningham had appeared at the drawing-room door. "What now?"

"No sign of him," said Gerald. "I said I'd walk down to the railway bridge; Uncle James is meeting me from his end. Perhaps he's hurt his leg or something."

Penelope caught Patience's eye. "We'll come too," she said. "Lucky we didn't change all the way." Although Mrs Cunningham was trailing a crimson hostess gown the two girls had compromised on short dresses after their days in tweeds.

"D'you think you'd better?"

"Of course we'd better," she cut him short. "Suppose he

45

is hurt? Someone's got to stay with him while we get the doctor."

"Yes, I suppose so." Gerald seemed reluctant to make such a practical admission of the worry that lay in all their minds.

Again the family rainwear was got out, but this time in haste and a preoccupied silence. Gerald picked up a large electric torch and they went quietly out the garden door.

Outside they stood for a moment blinking in the deep darkness of a moonless night.

"Look, Pen," said Gerald, "I think I'll go across the shortcut; he might have thought he was late and taken it – it's a bit tricky in the dark – you two take the big torch; I've got my pocket one." He disappeared into the darkness and they heard him rustling through the shrubbery by the summer house.

"Lord, it's dark," said Penelope. "You'd better hold my hand, Patience; I know the way." The torch picked out the orchard gate. "Be sure and shut it tight," said Penelope. "It's wired for rabbits. There goes one." They had both started at a sudden movement far too close to them in the bushes.

"Oughtn't we to call or something?" asked Patience as they closed the second gate. "He might have wandered off the path."

"Yes, I suppose we should." She paused for a minute, then raised her voice, "Father, cooee, *Father*. Can you hear me?" For a moment the silence closed deeper than ever, then, on the other side of the field, they heard Gerald's voice, a little tremulous, "Father, hi, Father," and then again the silence, ominous as when one knocks at an empty house.

They went on in silence until they got to the bottom of the field and saw, ahead of them, the wood looming darker out of the darkness. Penelope paused for a minute, the torch's light a very small patch of comfort on the ground ahead of them. "Perhaps we should call again," she said. "He might hear us now . . . Father, where are you?" Her voice sounded thin in the darkness.

Listening eagerly, Patience heard Gerald's voice ahead and to their right, "Hi, Father, where are you?" He did not sound as if he expected an answer.

"Let's hurry," said Penelope, "he's almost at the bridge; we don't want to miss him." They stumbled forward into the wood both silently convinced that Mr Cunningham was nowhere within earshot. An owl rose with a shriek. "I wish I could hear Uncle James," said Penelope. "But thank goodness, there's Gerald."

He was waiting for them where the shortcut joined their path. "Not a sign," he said grimly, and took their answer from their silence. "Well, come on." He led the way.

"Let's call again," said Penelope, mainly to be saying something. "Father, Father," her voice and Gerald's rose together and were joined by another one from ahead:

"Cunningham, Cunningham, can you hear me?"

"Thank goodness," said Gerald. "Uncle James. I can't see a thing."

But Patience had caught his arm. "Look," she said, "over there; in the bushes."

The thin beam of his pocket torch wavered towards the bushes at the side of the path, then stopped. "Pen," he said, "give me the big torch. No, you stay where you are." There was something in his voice that made them obey as he went on a few steps, torch in hand. They heard his whisper, "Oh, my God," as he bent down. Then he straightened up. "Uncle James," his voice shook, "he's here. Where are you?"

"I'm coming." The other voice was near now.

"Gerald, what is it? What's the matter with him?" Penelope was starting forward, but Patience caught her hand and held her.

"Pen, don't." There was a new note in Gerald's voice. "He's here . . . I think . . . he must be dead."

"*What*? Gerald?" Uncle James hurried up, the light from his torch joining Gerald's on the ground. "Good God," he knelt down. "You girls stay over there. Hold your torch a little lower, Gerald. No, I'm afraid there's nothing we can do. Poor old Albert; and all alone out in the dark like that. I never knew he had a weak heart." He stood up. "Gerald, you and I had better stay here while the girls go and get help. Penelope, you know what to do. Have your mother ring up Dr Hoblong and—" he paused, "yes, I suppose you'd better get Parkinson."

"Parkinson?" asked Penelope. He was the village constable.

"Yes, to give Hoblong a hand, you know. They'll need a stretcher."

Patience could feel that beside her Penelope was crying silently and steadily. "We'll do that," she said. "Come on, Pen."

"*Dead*?" said Mrs Cunningham. "Albert? It's impossible." She said it almost, Patience thought, with resentment. Then, "Parkinson and Dr Hoblong? Of course. I'll phone them; you'd better get Penelope to bed, she looks all in." She was the executive head of the Women's Institute, the manager of fêtes. She was, Patience thought, rather magnificent. She had said nothing, asked no questions; she was merely taking the necessary action.

From Penelope's bedroom she heard the calls. It was all very quick, very efficient; Dr Hoblong would call for Parkinson, who had only a bicycle. There was only one

48

surprising question, "Had you expected this, Dr Hoblong? Was there something he hadn't told me?"

After she had rung off for the second time there was silence for a few moments, then Patience heard the click as the receiver was lifted again. But Penelope was sitting up on her bed where she had lain since they got in. "I'm not going to bed," she said. "It's ridiculous. There'll be something to be done. Let's go downstairs. Poor Mother . . ."

"She's wonderful," said Patience.

Dr Hoblong was firm. "No, no, we shan't need you girls. We can find the way. Here, Parkinson, take the other end of the stretcher, would you?" Parkinson obeyed, the law bowing to medicine. He was a rubicund, middle-aged man, visibly horrified at this violent interruption of a life placidly devoted to being evaded by the village poachers.

After they left, Andrews had hysterics. It began with the soufflé, which was found, reeking, in the oven, and soon passed beyond any control but Mrs Cunningham's. While she was slapping her hands the front door bell rang. "Would you mind?" she asked Patience. "You make better sense than Penelope." In a corner of the kitchen, Penelope was sobbing silently, infected by Andrews.

A very young man in a dinner jacket stood at the door. In the blaze of light from the hall he looked fair, nervous and determined

"This is Hoblong's Hall? Good. I'm Colonel Forrester's nephew – the Chief Constable," he explained to Patience's baffled expression. "Mrs Cunningham called up about an accident."

"Oh, I see. Won't you come in?" How absurd the formality sounded

"Thank you." He looked once round the hall, hung his coat on the appropriate peg and said, "Are they back?"

"No, they only left five minutes ago."

The kitchen door opened and Mrs Cunningham appeared. Behind her, Andrews could be heard between sobs and laughter.

"Mr Crankshaw?" said Mrs Cunningham. "You're very young."

"I know. I'm sorry. I can't help it. How soon will they be back?" The final question dismissed the matter of his age once and for all.

"Oh, not for twenty minutes. Come in here, won't you?" They disappeared into the study.

"Who on earth is he?" asked Penelope who had emerged, red-eyed but calm, from the kitchen.

"Colonel Forrester's nephew. He says your mother called up."

"Mother? I wonder why."

"Colonel Forrester's nephew." Andrews, too showed signs of recovery. "Coo, he'll be the one who's just through police college. My boyfriend says—" she paused, wilted visibly, and dissolved into fresh floods of tears.

Patience and Penelope were still ministering to her when they heard the front door. "Here they are," said Patience. "Don't go, Pen." But they all three found themselves at the open kitchen door.

Major Balfour was holding both Mrs Cunningham's hands in his. "A frightful accident," he said. "You must be brave, Violet. These damnable poachers." Patience felt Andrews stiffen beside her.

"Poachers?" Mrs Cunningham looked up at him. "But I thought – Patience said – his heart?"

"No, I'm afraid not," Dr Hoblong paused. "You must be brave, Violet, as only you know how to be. I . . . I don't know how to tell you . . ." Was he, Patience wondered, horrified, was he perhaps enjoying the moment?

50

"What is it?" Mrs Cunningham looked from Hoblong to Balfour. "Tell me."

"It must have been quite sudden . . . You mustn't think he suffered." Hoblong was at his most unctuous. "But he was shot; shot through the head by some dastardly poacher." Scarlet with emotion, Hoblong made as if to wipe his brow, but discovered that he was still holding his end of the raincoat-draped stretcher. "We must take him upstairs. I wish I could have spared you this, Violet."

"You moved him?" The strange young man came forward from the study door.

"Course we moved him." Parkinson was suddenly authoritative. "Not going to leave poor Mr Cunningham out there in the cold all night. And who might you be, if I may ask?"

"Geoffrey Crankshaw. Colonel Forrester sent me. He sent you this." He handed a note to Parkinson whose face had crumpled comically as he spoke.

Oh, I see sir. Thank you sir." Parkinson managed to take the note with one hand and stuffed it into a jacket pocket. Slowly and laboriously he and Dr Hoblong got their load upstairs.

There was an agonising, expectant pause in the hall. After a minute, Major Balfour broke the silence. "Violet, you look ghastly. Hadn't you better get to bed? I'll take over now. Don't you worry about anything."

"I am sorry to be tiresome and officious," for all the apologetic words, there was something firm in Geoffrey's Crankshaw's voice. "But I think if Mrs Cunningham could stay a little longer, we might get some things cleared up. Perhaps we should all sit down and talk it over?"

Somehow they found themselves in the study. Geoffrey Crankshaw was at Mr Cunningham's desk, with the others in a half circle of chairs around him; pale, tired and, humiliatingly it suddenly occurred to Patience, starving.

Crankshaw looked at them. "By the way," he said, "have you had any supper?"

"*Supper*?" said Mrs Cunningham. "How can you talk of supper when my husband lies dead upstairs?" She paused magnificently and Patience noticed the return of self-dramatisation with relief. It was an unmistakable sign of recovery.

Crankshaw got up and they heard him at the kitchen door speaking to Andrews. "Coffee and sandwiches." However young, he had the gift of decision, thought Patience. "And the quicker the better." There was a strange silence. In the midst of it, Crankshaw seemed to be placidly thinking of other things but all the time, Patience felt, he missed not a movement of anyone in the room.

Mrs Cunningham was getting more and more restless. "Why don't you *do* something?" she burst out at last. "I told your uncle all about it. Isn't he going to do anything?"

"He sent me," said the young man mildly.

"That's all very well, but I know who did it. Isn't he going to be arrested or are we going to sit around here all night playing parlour games while Peter Everett gets clean away, document and all!"

"But," Penelope and Patience both spoke up at once, then were silent, looking at each other.

"Well?" Geoffrey Crankshaw encouraged Penelope.

"It's been returned; the document, I mean." She looked at her mother, who smiled with relief.

"And a good thing, too," said Major Balfour. "A lot of childish foolishness. But just the same, Crankshaw, Mrs Cunningham's right; I don't see why we're sitting around here talking while the scoundrel of a poacher who killed Cunningham gets away."

"Ah," said Geoffrey Crankshaw, "here come the sandwiches."

52

Dr Hoblong followed Andrews into the room and held a brief conference with Crankshaw while coffee was poured and sandwiches passed. Patience stole a glance at the clock: half past nine.

"Right." Dr Hoblong settled into a chair as Crankshaw called them to order. "First of all, however painful it is, I'm sure you'd like to know all you can about what happened. Dr Hoblong tells me that Mr Cunningham was killed by a bullet from what he thinks must have been a shotgun fired at fairly close range – about twenty yards, did you say, Doctor?"

"Thereabouts," said Dr Hoblong. "I wouldn't like to be too definite about it . . . the police surgeon . . ."

"Yes, of course. And you think he must have died between two and three hours ago."

"Yes, somewhere about then."

"But this is ridiculous," said Mrs Cunningham. "We all know when he died."

"Oh?" said Crankshaw.

"Of course. When that last shot was fired. You must have heard it in the study," she appealed to Penelope.

"Yes, yes we did," said Penelope. "Do you remember what time it was, Patience? It was when we had the doors open, remember?"

"Yes, so it was just after Andrews came in about the soufflé." Patience paused, "Yes, of course. You suggested we play piquet and I said wasn't it too late, and you said no, the clock was fast and the quarter-to-seven train was just going by?" She stopped, covered with confusion.

"Thank you very much, Miss Smith. Yes, I see, this clock is fifteen minutes fast," said Crankshaw, consulting his watch. "But what makes you think that particular shot was the one, Mrs Cunningham?"

"Oh, I don't know; I just thought . . ." she lapsed into confusion.

"Of course it was the one," said Major Balfour. "I mean it stands to reason, it was the làst one. Some poacher chap was firing around and when he saw what he'd done he cut and ran. You don't think he'd just go on with a quiet evening's rabbiting, do you?"

"What time did Mr Cunningham leave here?" Crankshaw did not mean to let the conversation get out of hand.

"Half past six," said Mrs Cunningham. "I remember because I was just going upstairs to lie down."

"And how long would it take to walk down to the railway line?"

"About a quarter of an hour." It was Gerald who spoke. "Unless he took the shortcut."

"But he said he wasn't going to," said Patience. "Don't you remember, Penelope? He said it was too wet."

"How long would it take by the shortcut?" asked Crankshaw.

"Oh, about seven minutes," said Gerald. "Hurrying, that is." His high colour had faded and he looked exhausted.

"I see. Well now, Mr Cunningham left here at half past six to walk over to your house, Major Balfour. You were expecting him at seven, is that right?"

"Yes, just after."

"And when he didn't arrive you wondered what had happened and called up here. What time would that be, I wonder?"

"Good Lord, let me think," said Major Balfour. "Do you remember, Gerald? About half past, I think. I thought perhaps he'd changed his mind about coming and I hadn't got the message. I've been in London all day, you know; I only got back on the seven o'clock."

"Oh, I see. And by half past you were naturally wondering if he was coming. So you talked to young Mr Cunningham," he smiled at Gerald in apology for the phrase.

"Yes. When he told me his father had left at half past six

54

I began to get rather anxious, but we thought Cunningham might have gone after the poachers; we've been having a lot of trouble with them lately – I expect your uncle will have told you – so I arranged to call again in ten minutes or so if he hadn't turned up."

"Which of course you did. That means that you all started out to look for Mr Cunningham at about quarter to eight, I take it. Who found him?"

"I did." Gerald was very white.

"I'll never forgive myself I wasn't quicker," said Major Balfour. "I might have spared you that, Gerald."

"But you got there right away," said Gerald, "thank God."

"Gerald!"

"I'm sorry, Mother."

There was an awkward silence, broken by Parkinson who put his head round the corner of the door. "We found it, sir," he said triumphantly. "Me and Bill. Right close to the path it was, like you said. Must have thrown it right away, I reckon. Bill's down there keeping an eye on things, but I brought it along, fingerprints and all, I hope."

"Good work." Crankshaw joined him for a minute in the hall, then returned to the expectant group in the study. "Yes," he said, "that'll be the gun all right; thrown in the bushes by the path, Parkinson says."

"Of course," said the Major. "Just what you'd expect some damn fool of a poacher to do. And now, Mr Crankshaw, perhaps you'll be so good as to let the ladies get to their beds. Personally, I'd like to know what right you think you have to keep us here asking a lot of silly questions when anyone can see Mrs Cunningham ought to be in bed."

"Yes, yes, of course," said Crankshaw soothingly, "but you know it was Mrs Cunningham who asked for me to come over."

"You, Violet?" His astonishment was almost comic.

"Yes, of course I did, James. Losing the document was quite bad enough – and naturally no one thought to tell me it had been returned – but when it came to losing poor Albert . . . of course I called Colonel Forrester. And it was very good of him to send his own nephew, too." She looked Crankshaw up and down. "But really, now we know it was just a horrible poaching accident, I don't believe we need trouble Mr Crankshaw any longer. It was very kind of you to come over, I'm sure." She was suddenly the hostess speeding an ill-timed guest.

"Not at all." Crankshaw fell obligingly into his role and looked at his watch. "Yes, it is getting late. But just before I go perhaps you'd all be so good – merely as a matter of form, of course, to tell me where you were between six-thirty and seven tonight. Mrs Cunningham?"

Mrs Cunningham drew herself up. "This," she said "is carrying things a little too far. You seem to forget, young man, that I am the dead man's widow." She paused impressively awaiting his apology.

He looked pinker and younger than ever but he stuck to his point. "Of course if you refuse," he said, "I can do nothing to compel you; I can only make a note of your refusal."

The Major intervened. "Come on, Violet; it's only common sense, really, the fellow's got to get the decks cleared. The quicker we answer him, the sooner he'll go out and catch the real villain – at least let's hope so."

Mrs Cunningham glanced quickly at her children. "Of course, if you insist," she said. "Let me think; yes, I went up to change as soon as your poor father had left, didn't I, and I lay down for a bit first – really, such an exhausting day – and I didn't come down till I heard you at the telephone, Gerald, talking to Uncle James."

Patience almost gasped. So Mrs Cunningham had blandly

56

suppressed her evening walk. She looked up quickly, caught Crankshaw's enquiring eye and felt herself go scarlet.

He took no notice however. "Thank you, Mrs Cunningham. Now," he looked at Gerald, "how about the rest of you?"

"I was in Camchester," said Gerald. "I went in on the six o'clock bus. Old Giles'll tell you I had to run to catch it."

"I see. And what time did you get back?"

"Just in time to take Major Balfour's call. We settled that was seven thirty, didn't we?" Gerald was almost too co-operative, Patience thought. But it did not last. At Crankshaw's next question his face closed. "Oh, I was just pubbing," he said. "I went to two or three – I don't suppose they'll remember me. I didn't do handsprings against the bar."

"No, I suppose not." Crankshaw was unperturbed. "The names of the pubs?"

"Let me see. The Railway Hotel – dreary joint but it's right by the bus stop; the Swan – someone was having a political row in the public so I didn't stay, and the Red Lion. The beer's terrible. Anything else you want to know?"

"Just how you got back. There's not a seven o'clock bus, is there?"

"Know everything, don't you? As a matter of fact I had a spot of luck and got a lift. I'd meant to take the eight o'clock but it meant being late for dinner, so when this chap said he was going to Cambridge I hitched a ride."

"So you had to walk up from the main road?"

"Yes, I can walk, you know."

But Crankshaw had turned away from him. "And you?" he asked Penelope.

"Miss Smith and I were here all the time till we went up to change – playing piquet mostly."

"I see. Did you see anyone else?"

"Andrews came in once." This time Patience was beyond

gasping. Clearly Peter Everett and Aunt Fan were not to be mentioned any more than Mrs Cunningham's walk.

Andrews was still dozing in the corner where Crankshaw had put her but looked up sharply when he spoke to her. "What did you come in for, Miss Andrews?"

"I wanted to ask about dessert."

"Oh. And you didn't ask Mrs Cunningham?"

A very intelligent look suddenly surprised Andrews' face. "I know better than to disturb her when she's lying down," she said.

"I see. And except for coming in here once you were alone in your kitchen? Is that right?"

"Dead right, sir."

"Good." He looked round the weary group. "Major Balfour we know was on the train from Camchester. How about you, Dr Hoblong?" The question came with surprising suddenness.

"Me?" He looked startled. "What's it got to do with me?"

Crankshaw smiled. "Oh well, we must be fair, you know. Can't leave you out after you've heard everybody else's confessions."

"Oh, I see. Let me think. There was a cricket club meeting at six-thirty – didn't last any time, though. Cunningham let us down rather." He looked embarrassed. "Supposed to have a report or something and never turned up. We broke up at once – we meet at the Feathers, you know, and I walked home. Got there about seven, I suppose. For once there were no calls so I sat down and read a book till Mrs Cunningham called."

"You live alone, don't you?"

"That's right. The exchange takes calls for me when I'm out. Oh, I see what you mean. No I can't prove when I got home, if that's what you're after. You'll just have to take my word for it."

58

"Right." He closed the diary in which he had been taking notes rather, Patience thought, at random. "You've been very patient with me, Mrs Cunningham, and now I don't think there's any reason why I should keep you up any longer. Get a good night's sleep if you can. I'll be around in the morning." His voice was part reassuring, part apologetic.

There was a general shuffling in the room. Andrews escaped into the hall, Dr Hoblong hurried over to speak to Mrs Cunningham and Major Balfour buttonholed Geoffrey Crankshaw. "Let me put you up for the night; you don't want to bother going all the way back to Forrester's place."

"Thanks very much." Crankshaw looked faintly surprised. "But I've arranged to stay at the Feathers . . . I'd better be getting along, too. They'll be waiting up for me. Good night, Mrs Cunningham."

His farewell was admirably brief, thought Patience, wishing that Major Balfour and Dr Hoblong would follow his example so that they could all go to bed. But they seemed to be trying to outstay each other, one on each side of Mrs Cunningham. Dr Hoblong offered her sleeping pills and Major Balfour moral support.

"Seems a nice enough young fellow, the policeman," he said. "I saw red at first at his keeping you all talking here, but I suppose he's got to do his job according to his lights. I rather wonder he didn't leave Parkinson on duty for the night – be sure you lock up well, Gerald my boy."

"It's all done," said Gerald stifling a yawn and the desire to add, "except the front door."

"That's the boy. Well, Violet, I must be getting along. Don't you worry about anything; I'll be over first thing in the morning and make all the arrangements. You won't have to do a thing. Glad the document turned up all right, by the way. I thought I was right about that."

"Oh yes." For a while Mrs Cunningham had actually been exhausted into silence but now she roused herself. "The Document. I suppose I'm never to know what goes on in my own house . . . making a fool of me in front of the police. When did you get it back and where is it anyway? Isn't anyone going to give it to me?"

"We put it back, Mother," said Penelope ignoring the first part of the question. "We thought you wouldn't want it opened till tomorrow. But of course that was before . . ." She began to cry again.

"Oh, Mother, haven't we had enough for tonight?" asked Gerald. "Let's all get to bed, for heaven's sake."

"Quite right, Gerald," said the Major, forestalling an outburst from Mrs Cunningham. "Hoblong, it's high time you and I were on our way and left these poor people to get some rest. See you in the morning, Violet. Take it easy, all of you."

"Thank God for that," said Gerald as he double-locked the front door behind them. "Now, Mother; bed. Take those pills and don't think about anything till the morning."

He sounded amazingly grown-up, Patience thought, after his undergraduate behaviour to Crankshaw. And it was good advice, too. The only trouble was that she found it impossible to take it. Fatally, she lay in bed thinking about it all, wondering if the others were having the same trouble and then going back, wearily, again and again, over the events of the day. A thousand years long, it seemed. And yet it was only after breakfast that the loss of the document had been discovered, and tomorrow was still Gerald's twenty-first birthday. What an odd creature Gerald was, so nice at times, but so maddening at others. The policeman seemed nice, for all his questions – had he spotted how they all lied to him? Did everyone always lie to the police?

What was the poacher thinking tonight, she wondered? Poor Mr Cunningham. But she did not want to think about him lying out in the cold wood as they had found him. She sat up in bed and switched on her bedside lamp. Three o'clock; she must have been asleep for a while after all. But now it was hopeless. She left the light on and picked up a book. Perhaps that would put her to sleep. But she could not concentrate on it. Queer the accident happening the day the document got lost. But it was safely back. Peter Everett must have been very near when Mr Cunningham was shot. You couldn't blame Penelope for keeping quiet about him. And what on earth were Mrs Cunningham and Aunt Fan doing out?

Her thoughts kept nagging back to the document. Something was bothering her about it. What was it? It had been on the edge of her mind earlier in the day when they were talking about it. She had it at last: they had never found the letter that explained about the document. You'd have thought Mr Cunningham would have kept the two of them together. Could they have overlooked it? Or did he keep it among the papers on his desk? Was that why he had been so cross about Giles looking at them? And what had Giles had on his mind at tea time? Not something about the letter, surely?

She was being ridiculous. There was no earthly reason why Giles should have had anything to do with document or letter. But where was the letter? It was no use. She had not a chance of getting to sleep now until she had had a look. Of course it was inquisitiveness and prying into other people's affairs and all that but she had long since learned not to waste time fighting her curiosity when once it got hold of her. She got up, put on a dressing-gown and opened her bedroom door quietly. Gerald had left the lamp on outside his mother's door in the hall below and it cast a dim light up into the second floor hall where she stood.

The house was silent. Everyone else must be asleep. Lucky things. She started downstairs, but paused outside Mrs Cunningham's door. Could she really be asleep? But of course, Dr Hoblong had given her something to take. She hurried past the next door, that of Mr Cunningham's room and on down the second flight of stairs. It was darker in the downstairs hall, but better not switch the light on.

She paused at the study door. Why not go back to bed? It was none of her business anyway. What nonsense; she was here now. She opened the door, felt for the light switch, and flicked it on. Nothing happened. She was surprised for a minute, then realised that the reading lamps must all have been turned off where they stood. It was always happening. She started to feel her way across the room to the lamp on the desk, then stopped, holding her breath. There was someone in the room with her. Now she was still she could hear the breathing, rather quick, rather deep.

Terror held her. If one of the others, why in the dark? But who else? And where were they? The room seemed huge, the distance back to the door immense. If only she had left it open. But they were moving, whoever they were, very quietly and towards her. Without thinking at all, she screamed and made a dash for the door. Someone passed just behind her and she heard the heavy curtains torn back. Screaming again (how odd to hear oneself do it) she found the hall light switch and turned it on.

The light was reassuring. Still more so was Gerald's voice. "What on earth's the matter?"

"Gerald, come quick." She could whisper now, remembering Mrs Cunningham. "There's someone in the study."

"In the study? Who?" He joined her, dishevelled with sleep.

62

"I don't know. The light's off at the door. I just heard them. Gerald, I'm frightened."

"You frightened? I don't believe it. I expect you dreamt it, anyway." But he hesitated a minute before he opened the study door. "Is anybody there?"

The hall light shone in a broad beam across the room and showed them the window curtain flapping in the wind.

"They've gone," said Patience. "I heard them at the window."

"Well, that's something." Gerald walked to the desk and switched on the light. The room was empty.

"But there was someone," said Patience. "Look at the window."

Gerald looked puzzled. "I could have sworn I locked them all." He looked at the catch. "No, it hasn't been forced. Funny."

Patience had been looking round the room. "Look," she said, "that's where he was." She pointed to the hearthrug which was crumpled against the fireguard as if someone had slipped on it. "I know that rug was straight when we went to bed. I was staring at it all evening."

"Good Lord," said Gerald. "The secret cupboard. Don't tell me the blessed document's been pinched again." But it was there, tucked away at the back of the cupboard where Penelope had left it earlier in the evening. "Good for you, Patience, you must have caught them in time."

Patience blushed with pleasure. "Oh," she said, "that reminds me of what I really came down for. Where's the letter, Gerald; the one explaining about the document?"

"Lord," he said, "I don't know. Tucked away somewhere I suppose. We'll have a look for it in the morning. But now I think you'd better get back to bed. I don't know what the neighbours would say if they found us wandering round the house at three in the morning. Or Mother for that matter."

Patience blushed again. "I see what you mean. But oughtn't we to do something about this?" She looked at the window.

"Oh, we'll tell that beautiful policeman in the morning. No sense spoiling his sleep. Whoever did it is in Muchton by now. I'll see you to your room."

Chapter Three

At the Three Feathers, Geoffrey Crankshaw ate a hearty breakfast and wished he was dead. Here he was, pitchforked by the kindness of his uncle into his first case, and already he had made a hopeless mess of it. Looked at in the gloomy light of morning his question session last night was nothing but a dismal parody of a detective story. And no doubt Major Balfour was perfectly right: all the time the poacher who had done it had been taking himself comfortably off to the next county.

Why had he done it anyway? Partly because they had all looked so unconscionably guilty sitting around in that depressing study (poor Mr Cunningham, he thought, in parenthesis). And partly, of course, because of his uncle's warning: 'they're a queer family the Hoblongs – Cunninghams now – something a bit fishy in the last generation. May be nothing in it, may not come out in this one; but keep an eye on them'.

He'd kept an eye all right. He helped himself savagely to more marmalade. And left Parkinson to find the gun. Of course he'd told him where to look, but it was thin comfort. Might as well face it. It had all been too romantic to be possible. Whoever heard of a first case so bristling with family secrets, missing documents and – for good measure – two beautiful girls. He caught himself thinking that of the two, Miss Smith was infinitely the more attractive, then pulled himself together. Enough of that. As penance, he would spend his morning in a sordid hunt for poachers.

Mrs Dudgeon, the landlady, had served his breakfast herself, her reason for the gesture amply clear in her inquisitive hoverings about him. Now, reassured that his tea was hot and his eggs to his liking, she came to the point. "Terrible business about poor Mr Cunningham," she said, hopefully.

"Yes, very sad." He had already learned that the less he talked the more other people did.

"Killed at once, they say. And as kind a man as ever took his pint. If I've said to Mr Dudgeon once, I've said it a thousand times, poaching ought to be a capital offence. But then in this village what can you expect?" She paused darkly.

"Oh?" He drank tea and looked encouraging.

"Well, perhaps I didn't ought to say it, you being connected with the police yourself and all, but you ask Bob Parkinson where his own wife's nephew was last night and I reckon you won't have much further to look. Those Pennyfolds have never been any better than they ought to be, even if Martha does do for the vicar – and gives herself enough airs about it, too, I can tell you. As if I wanted their unripe apples. But you're needing more hot water."

She bounced away to the kitchen, leaving him dazedly trying to disentangle the main heads of her speech. Obviously Mrs Parkinson's nephew would bear investigating, but where the vicar's apples came into it all was more than he could work out.

When she reappeared it was with a stiffened air. She put down the hot water, announced "Mr Parkinson's here," and retired, living up to her name.

Parkinson, too, was ill at ease and embarked without enthusiasm on the inevitable discussion of the local poachers. There were, he admitted, a group of lads who were not too particular whose rabbit they took from the snare or where they set their own snares. But guns, no. There'd been a bit of talk, recently, about shots down in Hoblong's Wood – the Major had been in to complain of them only a week or so before, but Parkinson refused to admit that this might be village boys. "Foreigners, it'll be," he said, "from Camchester, most like. The local boys are all right, I can tell you. Maybe they do take a rabbit they shouldn't from time to time; they're young, who wouldn't?"

"Or an apple?" asked Crankshaw.

Parkinson went scarlet in the face. "I knew it," he said. "That Mrs Dudgeon's been filling you up with a lot of stories about my wife's nephew. Well, perhaps he is a bit wild; but you can take my word for it, he never shot Mr Cunningham. Don't you waste your time on him, Mr Crankshaw."

"D'you know where he was last night?" asked Crankshaw. "I expect that'll settle it soon enough."

Parkinson looked uncomfortable. "Well," he said, "my wife did tell me her sister told her he was right at home drying the dishes for her." He paused.

"But you don't believe her?"

"Well, young Pennyfold's a nice boy, and I'd be the first to say so, but I just don't see him staying at home drying dishes for his mother." Parkinson was obviously relieved to have it off his mind.

"I see. Well, perhaps I'd better have a few words with young Pennyfold and settle where he actually was, and then we can really get down to things." Parkinson looked grateful at this suggestion that the interview with Pennyfold would be merely a matter of form. "Where do I get hold of him at this hour?"

"He'll be at the vicarage. He gardens there, Tuesdays and Thursdays."

Outside the vicarage Crankshaw paused. Would it be

polite to interrogate the vicar's gardener without first having a word with the vicar? One must, he felt, respect the formalities in a village like this. He rang the front door bell and asked a plump, slapdash woman who he assumed to be Mrs Pennyfold if he might see Mr Giles.

The vicar started when he was announced. Definitely a guilty start, thought Crankshaw with amusement; but he had taught himself to ignore this curious but general reaction to the appearance of the police. He explained, soothingly, that he wanted to speak to the vicar's gardener and thought that first . . . "Of course, of course," Mr Giles was himself again, "very nice of you. And now I wonder if there's anything I can do to help you over this shocking affair. Poor Mr Cunningham; a great loss to the parish, a very great loss."

"He was active in parish affairs, was he?" This was a new light on Mr Cunningham.

"Oh, most active; an invaluable man. The Football club, the Young Men's Club – a Churchwarden. I missed him sadly only this Sunday, but he had a bad cold, I believe, poor man. If only he'd stayed indoors yesterday, too. It was a poacher, I understand?" Even in the Church, curiosity raised its human head.

"Very probably. What about this wild group of boys they speak of in the village?"

"Young Pennyfold and his friends? Not a bit of real harm in any of them. Good boys, very good boys. Wildish of course; it's a hard time for the young, but no, you can rule them out, I'm sure. Young Pennyfold's worked for me ever since he came out of the Army and I wouldn't want a better boy. A bit ruthless in his digging, sometimes – only last week he dug up my—" The telephone interrupted him. "Excuse me – oh, yes, yes, he's here, just a minute – It's a call from Hoblong's Hall." He handed over the receiver and listened, curiosity rampant.

But the conversation was brief. "It looks as if I'll have to postpone my talk with young Pennyfold," said Crankshaw, replacing the receiver. "They've had a burglar at the Hall." Might as well satisfy the poor old man; after all, it would be all round the village in half an hour, if he knew Lesser Muchton. He said goodbye, got his car out of the shed behind the Feathers and picked up Parkinson who was pumping up a bicycle tyre, in obvious hope of a lift.

"Well," burst out Parkinson, as soon as the car started up again. "I've just had a word with young Pennyfold – gave him a bit of good advice, I did. 'Don't you try and hide anything from the police, Jim,' I said, 'it won't get you anywhere. There's Mr Crankshaw knows all about the vicar's apples already, and you'd better up and tell him what you were doing last night and no more talk about your mother's dishes either; it won't wash,' I said, 'Jim, and you know it won't'. And he came as clean as a whistle, Mr Crankshaw; I'm glad to say. Clean as a whistle."

Crankshaw congratulated him and elicited the details of young Pennyfold's confession with many pauses for further admiration of Parkinson's success in extracting it. Pennyfold, it seemed, had been courting the Cunninghams' maid, Andrews, for many years but she had been too comfortable in her position to want to leave it for a young man, who had, Parkinson admitted, a frivolous name in the village. Now, however, there was talk of his emigrating to America and this bait had made Andrews more cooperative. He had almost persuaded her on the Monday morning that she should come with him when Mr Cunningham appeared and ordered him off the place. Nothing daunted, he had returned at half past six, when he thought Mr Cunningham would be safely at the cricket club meeting, and had not left till seven – he didn't know last night that the bad time was quarter to," explained Parkinson, "or he'd have come

69

clean then. But who do you think he saw dodging about in the shrubbery when he left but Miss Fan – what was she doing out at that time of night I'd like to know? Have you thought about her at all, sir? She's crazy as a coot, you know; might do anything – and out wandering round in that trailing dress of hers in all the rain last night. Mighty funny, it sounds to me." But they had arrived at Hoblong's Hall and Crankshaw had hardly time to be properly impressed by this suggestion.

They found the whole party, including Major Balfour who had just arrived, assembled in the study. When Crankshaw appeared everyone turned to him at once. "I thought you were coming round first thing in the morning," said Mrs Cunningham reproachfully. "Here we are, practically murdered in our beds, and not a bit of police protection do we get." The variations on this theme lasted for some time and Crankshaw apologised as best he might while he listened to the description of the night's events that was being poured out by Gerald and Patience.

When they paused for breath, he summed up. "So you disturbed him in here, Miss Smith, and you think he was after the document in the secret cupboard?"

"That's it." In the light of day, Patience was rather enjoying her night's terror. She explained about the fireside mat. "But the document's still there," she finished, "so I must have caught him in time."

"And what is this document?"

"That's just what we don't know." Gerald explained briefly about the document's origin, with many interruptions and lamentations from his mother.

"I see," said Crankshaw finally. "And this is the day it's to be opened?" Gerald nodded. "Well, then, with your permission, Mrs Cunningham, I think we should open it right away."

"What?" said Mrs Cunningham, "Not wait for the Dinner?"

"Good Lord, Mother," said Gerald, "You know we can't have a party now."

"Oh, very well," said Mrs Cunningham. "Have it your own way. Of course it doesn't matter that it's an occasion I've been looking forward to for twenty years. But there's no one left who cares about my feelings now."

This unfair appeal was made directly at the Major, who promptly let her down. "Splendid idea," he said to Crankshaw. "Should have been opened long ago, if you ask me; then there wouldn't have been all this mystification and bother. Go to it, Gerald."

Gerald glanced apologetically at his mother and opened the secret cupboard. "Here it is," he said, taking out the small package with its many seals.

"Just a minute," said Crankshaw. "D'you mind if I take a look before you open it?" He looked the packet over carefully, then silently returned it to Gerald. "Right, go ahead."

"I'm sorry, Mother." Gerald broke the seals and took out a long sheet of paper. A curious look came over his face. "But," he said, "this can't be it; it must be the letter Uncle Gerald sent. Unless it's all some kind of a hoax. What fools we'd look." He was quickly reading through the letter as he spoke. "Yes, it's the letter all right. But where on earth's the document?" He handed the letter to Crankshaw, who pitied the curious group and read it aloud.

" *'Dear Albert,*
I hope you'll be sorry to hear that I'm dying, but anyway, whether you're sorry or not, there it is. And out at the back of beyond, too, with not even a drop of whisky to cheer me up to face it. But I expect I'll manage

all right when it comes to the point; I sometimes think we've managed worse things than that in our time.

Give my love to Fan, if she understands anything these days, and to Violet, of course. She'll weep buckets for me, that's one good thing. Out goes the last of the Hoblongs, and good riddance, if you ask me.

Still, I'm glad you've got a boy. There are better names than Gerald, but he's welcome to it, such as it is. I'll be sending him a 21st birthday present one of these days, before I lose my grip altogether; but I want it to get to you safely and it'll take a bit of arranging. It's just a bit of paper, but keep it for him till he's 21 and you might find it was worth something to him.

Well, goodbye; I wish I was safely dead.

Gerald.'

"Then there's a postscript," said Crankshaw, and read it:

'You'd never guess who's just turned up, not that I feel very hospitable on my deathbed, but he'll do to take the document for Gerald. Or will he? Perhaps I'll give him this and let him think it's the document. Why should one trust anyone after all? And I'll seal them both with my signet ring – you remember it – and throw it in the lake afterwards à la King Arthur. It's the only one now so you'll know if anyone fools around with the papers. But after all, why should he?'

"And that's the end," said Crankshaw. "I wonder who his visitor was."

"Wonder, indeed," said Mrs Cunningham. "If you're wondering, you might wonder where the document is."

72

"It is odd," said Gerald. "I could swear that this was the packet that's been there all the time, couldn't you, Pen?"

"I'd have said so," said Penelope. "What d'you think, Uncle James?"

"I don't know, my dear; I never saw one nor t'other. I'm about the only person in Muchton who hasn't, I should think."

"You never saw the letter and the document together?" Crankshaw asked the young Cunninghams.

"No, it's queer, you know; we never did. Father always said the letter was put away when we asked to see it, and it would be time enough when Gerald was twenty-one. You know the kind of thing," said Penelope.

"I see. So the document may actually have been missing for years?"

"Oh no," again it was Penelope. "Father would have told us. But it is queer; I see what you mean. If it was only the letter in here, why was he so upset when it was pinched?"

"Exactly. And now I think it's time we got it straight about the disappearance of the document – if it was the document. When exactly was it found to be missing?"

"Yesterday morning," said Gerald. "Good Lord, it seems like years. Father found it was gone, didn't he, Mother?"

"Yes, he came fussing in to me first thing – said he'd found it was missing overnight, but hadn't wanted to worry me, or something."

"And he'd spent all Sunday in the study with his cold," put in Gerald, "so we knew it must have been taken Saturday night or sometime Saturday."

"When had it been last seen?" asked Crankshaw.

"That's what's so tiresome," said Mrs Cunningham, ignoring Penelope's appealing glance. "That miserable girl, Penelope, said she and Patience had seen it at six o'clock and all the time they hadn't."

"I see." Crankshaw looked carefully anywhere but at Penelope. "So we don't really know when it was last seen."

"I think Father saw it last," said Penelope. "After I told him we hadn't really seen it that night he said something about knowing it was there Saturday morning. He said he put it there himself, or something."

The Major had been turning slowly purple. "D'you mean to tell me that you told us all a wilful lie just to shield that young scamp of a Peter Everett?" he turned on Penelope.

"It was only a joke," said Penelope.

"A pretty serious sort of a joke as it's turned out, I'm afraid." Crankshaw did not mean to lose control of the conversation. "Now, I think perhaps, Miss Cunningham, you'd better tell us all about this business of young Everett and the document."

"But it wasn't the document." Penelope wailed. "It was *this*," she pointed to the letter. "He took it when he came over from the flower show to tidy up after he caught the greasy pig."

Crankshaw caught Mrs Cunningham's stony eye and hurriedly suppressed a smile. "Oh, and what did he do with it?"

"That's what's so frightful. It was here all the time. He hid it under a loose board we found when we were children."

"I see. And how did you discover it in the end?"

"He came and told us." Penelope was suddenly scarlet.

"When?" The word fell cold.

There was a silence. Then Gerald spoke up. "Come on, Pen, this is serious. And you know perfectly well Peter can't have had anything to do with it."

"No, of course not. I was silly." She looked at Crankshaw. "He came just after half past six last night."

"Did he? And how long did he stay?"

74

"I – I don't really remember." Her confusion was obvious.

"I see. He left before you heard the shot. Is that it? Perhaps you remember, Miss Smith?"

"Yes, just before, I think." Patience looked apologetically at Penelope. "But really, you can't possibly think . . ."

"I'm not thinking anything at all," said Crankshaw. "I'm just trying to get a few facts straight. Now let's see. Peter Everett arrived here just after half past six – after Mrs Cunningham had gone upstairs to change, I take it – and he stayed for a few minutes; just long enough to remind you about the loose board. Why did he go so soon, by the way?"

"He thought he heard Mother coming," said Penelope desperately.

"Oh? I understood Mrs Cunningham was upstairs till Major Balfour phoned?"

"Yes, that's quite right," said Penelope, (so she's sticking to that lie, thought Patience), "it turned out to be Andrews, not Mother."

"But anyway, Everett left. Which way did he go?"

"Out the window – the way he came."

"And his shortest way home would be across the valley to Lesston." Crankshaw had learnt a lot about the geography of the district in the course of the day. "Did he usually go by the path or the shortcut?"

"The shortcut, usually," said Gerald reluctantly.

"So what's worrying you all is that he might have got down to the railway line by the time your father was shot. Is that it?"

"He'd have had to hurry like anything," said Penelope. "Don't you remember, Patience? It was no time at all, really. Andrews came in about Mother and we opened the windows and we heard the shot right away."

Patience looked quickly at Mrs Cunningham and realised as she did so that Crankshaw was watching her. "Why did you open the windows?" he asked.

There was a brief pause. Then, "To see if we could hear the train go by," said Penelope. "We were wondering if there was time for some piquet before dinner. You remember, we told you; it's why we know what time the shot was." Well saved, thought Patience, and was again uncomfortably aware of Crankshaw's eye on her.

But to her relief he changed the subject. "I wonder if I might have a word with Miss Hoblong?" he said to Mrs Cunningham. "If she's well enough today, that is."

"With Fan? What a ridiculous idea! As if she could possibly have anything to do with it." But there had been an uncomfortable stirring in the room. "Besides," went on Mrs Cunningham, "I'm not at all sure she's well enough. And after all, it isn't as if it was the gun." There was a gasp from Penelope and she stopped short, looking horrified.

"What wasn't the gun?" asked Crankshaw.

"Oh, Mother," said Gerald. "It's nothing really," he turned to Crankshaw. "It's just that Father said he found Aunt Fan wandering round yesterday with his old sporting gun. But it's back in its place, I looked."

"I'm sure you did," said Crankshaw. "It's a pity you didn't tell me about it sooner. Would you mind showing Parkinson where it is. And watch out for fingerprints, Parkinson, though of course it's far too late."

"But you've got the gun already," said Major Balfour.

"Can't be sure it's the one," said Crankshaw. "I hope I'll be hearing from Camchester about it any time now." He turned to Mrs Cunningham. "And now we've got that cleared up, perhaps I could see Miss Hoblong."

Mrs Cunningham looked flustered and Major Balfour

intervened. "You know," he said. "It's none of my business, of course, but poor old Fan isn't too good right now – the children will tell you – mightn't it be a good idea to have the doctor along to keep an eye on her – you know, make sure she doesn't get too upset or anything? After all, she doesn't even know about poor Albert, does she?"

"Yes," said Mrs Cunningham, obviously relieved. "Yes, of course that's the thing to do. Dr Hoblong's coming to see her tomorrow morning; if you wouldn't mind waiting till then, Mr Crankshaw, I do think it would be a great deal better. Really, I've got enough on my hands without having poor Fan thrown into hysterics by having to answer a lot of questions." It was so obviously, though absurdly, true, that there was nothing more to be said.

Crankshaw rose as Parkinson reappeared with a long, awkward brown paper parcel. "Got it? Right, we'd better be going. I'll ask Camchester to send out a couple of men to keep an eye on things for you, Mrs Cunningham, just in case your burglar comes back. But let's hope Miss Smith's frightened him off for good. Very nice going it was too," he spoke directly to Patience for almost the first time. "Not many girls would have had the courage."

"It wasn't courage," Patience blushed. "I was terrified. I don't know what I'd have done if Gerald hadn't come along."

Driving back to Parkinson's office, Crankshaw decided that he must try to get a few words alone with Miss Smith. She looked as if she could fill in a good many of the curious pauses in the Cunninghams' evidence if he could only persuade her to. Besides . . . he suddenly found himself unaccountably annoyed with Gerald for coming to her aid in the night.

A large and prosperous-looking police inspector was waiting

77

for them in the tiny office that took the place of a living-room in Parkinson's house.

"Ha," he said. "Here you are at last. Been out solving the case I suppose. Colonel Morrison told us he'd put you on to it – bit unusual, of course – so I've come over to keep an eye on things. Inspector Adams, the name is. Can't let you have all the fun. Been up at Hoblong's Hall, I hear. You didn't bring the murderer back with you?"

Crankshaw laughed. "No, not quite yet," he said. "We had an interesting morning, though."

"Well now," Inspector Adams had settled himself comfortably in the one easy chair, "let's hear all about it. Poaching accident by all accounts. Where was this young Pennyfold they speak of at the time?"

"Well, as a matter of fact, it looks rather as if he's got an alibi." Crankshaw explained about the visit to Andrews.

"Hmmm. Alibi provided by the girlfriend. All very convenient but I don't take much stock in it myself. I suppose you've been all over the scene of the crime."

"Parkinson has." Crankshaw felt suddenly that he had been deplorably remiss.

"Ah. While you were at the Hall, no doubt. He found the gun, I hear. Very nice work." If a policeman can, Parkinson purred. "Well, I think that's the place to start. Let's have a look where you found it." Adams rose, six broad feet of determination.

But there was something on Crankshaw's mind. It had lain there since he left Hoblong's Hall and now stirred uncomfortably. "You know," he said, "before we go; I wonder if there oughtn't to be someone on duty at the Hall. I don't like the feel of things up there – I told Mrs Cunningham she should have someone for tonight," he explained about the burglary, "but I've got a feeling there ought to be someone there now."

78

Adams guffawed. "Feelings," he said, "you've got a feeling! Let me tell you, my lad, we don't run this police force on feelings, we run it on hard work, and hard work is what you're going to do this afternoon. When you're as old as I am you'll know that people get so worked up once they've been involved in anything violent that they see burglars in every bush. I'm as sure as I stand here that that girl imagined the whole business last night. It stands to reason: no one in their senses would burgle the Hall; it wouldn't be worth the walk from the village. And as for their document . . ." Another guffaw finished the sentence. But he saw that Crankshaw still looked worried and went on more kindly, "Don't you worry about them, they'll be all right. We'll put someone on duty there tonight, since you promised, but this afternoon you're going to help me look for clues in Hoblong's Wood. You can tell me all you've done over lunch and then we'll get to it. Lots of intelligent questions you've asked, I've no doubt, and not done much solid work; but never mind, you'll learn."

They left Parkinson behind with instructions to try and get in touch with Peter Everett, and set out by the village path to Hoblong's Wood. "Though I'm sure young Everett's got nothing to do with it," said Adams. "Just a private spite against Mrs Cunningham – you don't want to let that business about the document mix you up, my boy; pure coincidence, that's what it is."

"It's funny though," Crankshaw protested. "The real document's still missing – almost looks as if it always had been and Mr Cunningham wasn't letting on."

"Probably never was a document," said Adams wisely, "and he didn't dare to tell his wife."

"Oh," said Crankshaw, as an idea struck him, "yes, there might be something in that." But they had reached the wood, and Adams put him to work looking for traces of poachers before he could pursue it further.

The place was damp and bedraggled with September rain. The erratic paths of blackberry pickers and rabbits criss-crossed it here and there and they followed them systematically between the path and the railway line. Before long they had a considerable collection of used cartridges and cigarette ends, all of them old and sodden, and two ancient and deplorable handkerchiefs. Presently they reached the spot just beside the path where the body had been found and, near by, Parkinson's red handkerchief in the bushes where he had found the gun. "Yes," said Adams, "just what I expected. See, he was shooting from these bushes across the path to that warren – Mr Cunningham comes by unexpectedly, and there you are. He drops his gun and bolts – back across the railway line for a bet. Let's have a look."

As they struggled through the sloe and blackberry bushes which grew thickly at this point Crankshaw said, "But wouldn't he have heard him come? He must have been so close to the path. I don't see how he could have helped but hear."

"Not in all that wind and rain last night," said Adams. "The last thing he'd expect would be someone out on a night like that. I know what's the matter with you, you want a good glamorous murder; a poaching accident's not fancy enough for you. But you mark my words, my boy, be grateful for something simple to begin on. And look here—" he broke off triumphantly as they reached the wire fence that marked off the railway embankment. A faint but unmistakable path led from where they stood through a loose section of fence and down on to the railway line. "Someone used this way to come on his outings," said Adams. "Come on." Crankshaw paused to remove a tiny piece of fluff from one of the barbs of the wire and Adam's voice came excitedly down to him from the top of the embankment. "What are you doing up there? Look what I've found." He sounded, thought Crankshaw, as he climbed down through the thick shrubbery of the embankment, like an excited child hunting shells at the seaside. When he reached the bottom he found Crankshaw peering into a dilapidated working men's hut. "Can't have been used since they repaired the line last," said Adams, "and that was before the war – and just look at that path."

It was quite true. The faint path they had been following became suddenly more definite and led straight into the shack. Adams bent to look at the rusty padlock that secured the door and let out another cry of triumph, "What d'you think about that?" Wrapping his hand in his handkerchief he removed the padlock, which was merely closed and not locked, and opened the door. Inside there was a jumble of broken tools, old socks and wooden boxes, dimly visible in the light from the door. "Someone's been here all right," said Adams, "and often too." He shone his torch on the well beaten earth of the floor and Crankshaw picked up three cigarette stubs and an empty matchbox. "Woodbines," said Adams, "what you'd expect. I suppose you're still hoping for some cigar stubs left by a villain in a high-powered car." Crankshaw said nothing. Adams had been at him on these lines all afternoon and though it was kindly meant he was beginning to find it wearing. Besides, he was worried about the family at Hoblong's Hall; there had been something in the air that morning, it was more than just a feeling. He was sure of it. But what had it been; who had it come from? He racked his brains in vain. There had been high tension in the room, but who had generated it he had no idea. He must get back there as soon as he could; perhaps Miss Smith would have felt it too. She was out of it, all right, and seemed level-headed enough for anything.

Adams was digging like a terrier among the boxes and

sacks. "Lots of meals been eaten here," he said. "Look." Proudly, he held up an empty sardine tin and bovril jar. "No caviare, I'm afraid."

Crankshaw's worry broke out, "Yes," he said, "so they have. But don't you think perhaps we ought to be getting back to the Hall? It'll be dark in an hour or so."

"And what of it? I suppose you want to get back and protect them from Cunningham's ghost. I don't know what else they've got to worry about. Listen." He broke off and they both listened, breathless.

Faint but unmistakable, cautious footsteps were approaching down the railway; for a while they would be inaudible, then would come the crunch of gravel as a foot slipped off the sleepers. Silently, Adams pulled the hut door to and they crouched in the corner among the boxes, their only light a thin beam from round the edge of the door.

The footsteps came nearer and paused outside the hut. Then the door swung open and Crankshaw saw a solid young man outlined against the light outside. He hurried in and shut the door behind him, then shone a small flashlight into the corner opposite them where the broken tools were piled. With a smothered exclamation he began turning over the tools.

"Looking for something?" asked Adams, turning his own powerful flashlight on.

He jumped, turned and faced them, blinking in the strong light. "I won't say a word," he said. "So help me I won't say a word; not to save my life. Oh, it's you, Mr Crankshaw." There was no doubting the relief in his voice.

"Yes. And you're Jim Pennyfold, I take it." Crankshaw risked it.

"Yes, sir, that's me. And Lord, I'm glad it's only you."

"Who did you think we were?" Adams had opened the door, letting the dwindling evening light in on the party.

"Why, him, of course."

"Who?"

"Him, who done him in, Mr Cunningham, I mean."

"Who's that?" The question came sharply.

"How should I know. Lor', you frightened me, I thought I was done for. I wouldn't have wanted to meet him here; lor'," he said again, still visibly shaken.

"And why should you have?" Adams was piling in his questions as fast as possible, but Pennyfold was pulling himself together. He paused before answering, "Well, it's so near where it happened," he said, unconvincingly.

"Come now, you know that's not the reason. What do you know about this hut and what were you looking for just now?" Even while they were talking Pennyfold had been darting eager glances into the corner as if in hopes that the daylight would reveal whatever it was he had been looking for. Again he hesitated.

"Come on, you'd better tell us, unless you want to be taken up as an accessory. I don't think much of that alibi of yours either; I've been looking for you already."

Pennyfold wilted before Adams' menacing tone. "I was looking for the gun," he said. "It's gone. It must have been it."

Unravelling this somewhat cryptic statement by further questioning, Adams elicited that Pennyfold and a group of his friends had used this hut as a hiding and meeting place ever since they were boys. It was clear – though he slid over it as best he might – that in more recent times it had been extremely convenient as a centre for poaching operations; standing as it did, between Major Balfour's land and Hoblong's Wood. Handling this tactfully, Adams managed to bring a now balking Pennyfold to confess that one of them – he refused to name him – had got hold of a shotgun which had been hidden in the corner of the hut so that any of them who was tired of setting illicit snares – their usual occupation – and who could get hold of some ammunition, could have a shot with it. Pennyfold's first thought, when he heard of Cunningham's death, had been of the gun and he had been unable to restrain his anxiety to see if it was still in its place.

"Much better to have come along to the police station," said Adams, "the way you're going to now, and identify the gun Mr Cunningham was killed with; though it's your friend's, beyond any doubt. Come on now."

They set out at a brisk pace down the railway line and as they went Adams succeeded in browbeating the names of his associates out of Pennyfold. There were four others: two from Lesser Muchton, one from Lesston and one – the owner of the gun – from Camchester.

"Should be easy enough to check up on them," said Adams, ignoring Pennyfold's protestations in their defence. "And you're sure no one else knew about the gun's being there."

"Not a soul, sir. They'd have made trouble for us soon enough; there's a lot of interfering old women in this village. If anyone'd got on to it it'd have been all round the place directly." Pennyfold was cheering up somewhat as he found that he was not put under immediate arrest.

"Anyone seen you out with the gun?" asked Crankshaw.

"Never. Oh," he paused, "come to think of it, I did run into Miss Hoblong one day; but of course it didn't matter about her, poor old thing. Half the time she doesn't make sense anyway. She just looked at me, said one of those queer things of hers, and went on picking flowers."

Crankshaw's anxiety came to a head. "I'm worried about her," he said to Adams. "You saw her last night, didn't you Pennyfold?"

"Yes, sir. Dodging about in the shrubbery, she was, when

I went round to the back door. About half past, it'd have been. I don't know what they're thinking of, letting her out in that rain."

Adams was interested at last. "Which way was she going?" he asked.

"Down towards the river. She's often down at Hoblong's Bridge, you know. That's where she saw me, that time. Of course, I wasn't doing anything *with* the gun," he hastened to add. "Just playing around."

"Nothing to do with Major Balfour's pheasants, of course," said Adams. "Well, anyway, she wasn't going towards the Lesston path." He sounded almost as relieved as Crankshaw felt. "I think maybe you're right, Crankshaw," he went on and the concession was a considerable one. "The sooner we get a couple of men on guard at the Hall the better."

Chapter Four

At Hoblong's Hall the day had dragged. Major Balfour stayed to lunch, but went home immediately afterwards, complaining that one of his bouts of malaria was coming on. Mrs Cunningham retired to bed with a hot water-bottle and the young people resumed what had already become a hopeless search for the missing document. They were interrupted by the front door bell and Penelope, who had been dragging out the contents of the cupboards under the bookcase in the study, leapt to her feet. "Thank goodness," she said, "it'll be Peter."

"It's certainly time he turned up," said Gerald, "but he'd come by the window, wouldn't he?"

Andrews looked into the room. "Dr Hoblong's here," she said. "I told him Mrs Cunningham was in bed, and he wants to see you, Miss Pen."

"Oh Lord," Penelope pulled a face.

"Better see him, Pen," said Gerald. "And do get him to take a look at Aunt Fan. She was talking about the deaths of kings when I took her lunch up."

"He's in the drawing-room." Andrews had lingered at the door.

"All right, I'll go." Penelope rose, pushed her hair back from her forehead with a dirty hand, made a face at herself in the mirror and left the room.

Gerald closed the last of the desk drawers with a bang.

"It's not here," he said. "I knew it wasn't."

Patience was working her way systematically along the books in the shelves, making sure nothing was hidden behind them. "No," she said, "I'm sure it's not here at all. Gerald, do you really think it has anything to do with your father?"

"I don't know what to think," said Gerald. "I wonder if the document got lost some time ago and Father didn't like to tell Mother . . . that might be it, you know."

"Yes, I suppose it might. But then what d'you think was the matter with Mr Giles. He was in such a queer state yesterday afternoon – and where was your father all afternoon? Was it like him to go off like that and not tell anyone? I shouldn't have thought it was."

Gerald hesitated. "He said something to Pen when he got back. Did you hear him?"

"About looking for Peter Everett? Yes, I did. I thought he was off in his boat somewhere."

"Yes, he is. But you know how it is round here; he might be up any of the inlets – he often comes up to Small Harbour, I know. It's only five miles across country; Father might have walked it. I wish to goodness we'd asked him."

Patience had been thinking. "Gerald," she said at last, "don't you think you really ought to tell Mr Crankshaw everything? About your mother being out, you know – and Mr Giles, of course. And," she hesitated for a moment and then went bravely on, "and did you really tell him all you'd been doing in Camchester? It didn't sound quite right somehow, and I saw him make a note in that little book of his. I'm sure it'd be much better to tell him. If he knows everything he won't have to waste a lot of time with ridiculous enquiries about you. And of course as long as you don't tell him things, you can't expect . . ." she paused, furious to find herself blushing.

Gerald got up angrily. "Of course, if you want to go and

87

tell tales to the police," he said, "we can't stop you, but I really don't see what affair it is of theirs if I happen to meet a friend in Camchester and Mother wants to go out for a walk."

"But at half past six at night? You know there must have been something odd about it."

"She went to look for Aunt Fan." Gerald still spoke angrily. "She said so."

"Of course you weren't there," Patience blushed harder than ever, "but really, she sounded odd as could be when she came in. And would she really go out after Miss Hoblong? Wouldn't she get one of you to go?"

Gerald gave in. "I'm sorry, Patience. Of course you're quite right; but the whole business is getting me down. I don't know what to do. And you can't think Mother had anything to do with it."

"No, no of course not. That's just the point. I'm afraid Mr Crankshaw's going to waste a lot of time trying to find out if you really went to Camchester and it seems so silly. And you can't tell, it might help to know what your mother was doing. It would clear things up a bit anyway. I don't see how the police can get anywhere when everyone tells them lies. I'm sorry, Gerald," she saw his frown, "but you know you all did."

Before he could answer, Penelope burst into the room. Her hair was untidier than ever and her eyes were red. "How could he!" she said. "The day after Father . . ." The sentence ended in a flood of tears.

"What on earth's the matter, Pen," Gerald put an awkward arm around her while Patience silently handed her a handkerchief to replace her own sodden one.

"He asked me to marry him, the beast." In her fury, Penelope sounded like an angry schoolgirl. "And when I said 'no' he came over and put his horrible fat hand on my shoulder and said I'd better because I wouldn't be likely to get another chance after the scandal we're in for . . . He said I ought to be grateful to him for coming back. Oh, he was horrible. And he was sure I'd have him: he had his best suit on and the worst tie of all – the one with the nudes, Gerald – all ready to celebrate. And talking about a scandal, just because poor Father . . ." A flood of tears stopped her.

"Scandal?" said Gerald angrily. "What on earth does he mean? Where is he now, Pen? D'you want me to see him?" Unlike Penelope, he sounded very much the grown-up.

"Up with Aunt Fan. No, leave him alone, Gerry. I hate him; I told him so."

"Good for you."

"And he said I'd be sorry for it one day and not so far off either, but I needn't think he'd ask me again. There were as good fish in the sea – he really said that, wasn't it priceless?" Laughter began to mingle, somewhat hysterically, with the tears.

"There he goes," said Gerald. "He didn't stay with her long." They were silent, listening to Dr Hoblong's heavy, self-confident footfall on the stairs.

"Thank goodness," breathed Penelope, as they heard the front door close with its heavy bang. "Oh, please, do let's stop talking about it all, I can't stand any more." She was still very close to tears.

Gerald had an inspiration. "I know," he said, "let's walk over to Small Harbour. Peter might be in there by now; he likes the pub there, I know."

Penelope brightened up at once. "I say, that's a wonderful idea. Are you coming, Patience? It's five miles." She sounded doubtful of Patience's capacity for the distance.

She might have known better, thought Gerald, as they started off at a good stride through the village. By unspoken consent they had avoided the shortcut across the valley, even

89

though this put an extra mile onto their walk. Even so, they reached Small Harbour by four o'clock, only to see, at one disappointed glance, that there was not a boat in the muddy inlet. "Still," said Gerald, "let's leave a message. He may come in any day. They won't mind our knocking them up at the pub." Suiting the action to the word, he beat resoundingly on the closed door of the tiny inn that looked out over the harbour.

"What's the matter?" A bedraggled female head looked out of an upstairs window. "Oh, it's you, Mr Cunningham. No, he baint here today any more than he was yesterday. What's the fuss about anyway? I told your father I'd have him get over to Great Harbour and phone as soon as he did come in. Thinks I'm losing my memory, I suppose." There was a little gasp of silence as her audience realised that she had not yet heard of Mr Cunningham's death.

"Sorry we've bothered you again," Gerald pulled himself together. "But we do want to get hold of Mr Everett. Here, have a drink on us when you open up." He pushed something that rattled through the rusty letter-box and the head took on a more benevolent appearance.

Encouraged by this, Patience put in a question she had been wanting to ask. "What time did Mr Cunningham get here yesterday? We never thought he'd make it," she explained.

"What time? Round about this time, I reckon. I know, I was asleep then, just the way I was now. Yes," she considered for a minute. "I heard the four-thirty siren from Camchester just after he left – proper wet he was too, poor man, don't know why they went telling him Mr Everett was here – ain't seen him nor heard of him since Easter. And why they have to go letting those sirens off when there's no need, as if we hadn't been terrified enough by them, is what I'd like to know."

Gerald agreed with her, apologised again, and repeated his message for Peter Everett. "Tell him it's urgent, would you?"

The head looked wise, grinned at Penelope and was still nodding as they turned and started back down the road round the harbour.

"Bright of you to think of asking when he got here," said Gerald to Patience. "It works out about right, actually . . . he can't have left home till about three, just the way we did, so he would get here about the same time."

"Yes, of course," said Patience. "But didn't he take rather a long time getting back? I mean if it took him an hour and a quarter to get over; why an hour and a half to get back – more, really? She said he left here before four-thirty, and he wasn't back till after six, was he?"

"No, that's true" said Penelope. "More like quarter past, it was. And he's a fast walker." She stopped for a minute; then went on rapidly. "D'you think he could have gone somewhere else too, to look for Peter?"

"There's nowhere else he could have got to in the time," Gerald reminded her. "Great Harbour's a couple of miles further on and he'd never have made that. He might have stopped and asked Mrs Everett, I suppose, but it doesn't seem likely somehow."

"Gerry," Penelope paused to look back at the harbour, cold and grey in the flat calm of evening, "couldn't we go over to Great Habour? He really might be there. It's not really quite as much as two miles."

Gerald looked at his watch. "Honestly, Pen, I don't think we should. After all, poor Mother . . ."

There was no getting away from it, and they walked on in silence and at a good conscience-stricken pace. But Penelope, who had refused to change her shoes to come out, developed a blister on her heel which slowed her to a bad-tempered hobble behind the others. Serve her right for thinking Patience couldn't make it, thought Gerald, in a moment of brotherly irritation as he urged her on. "We really must be home by six, Pen. Mother's going to be wild enough about tea, without having to pour her own sherry."

But it was six o'clock when they reached Lesston. Gerald looked at the girls. "We'd better take the shortcut," he said. "We've got to do it sometime, after all."

"We could go round by Hoblong's Bridge," said Penelope. "It's not much further."

"That's a good idea — and if we sneak into the house through the shrubbery we might get away with it. The bridge is on the old river road from Muchton to Lesston," he explained to Patience. "It was the main road in the 19th century, but it's been closed since the Camchester road was put through. It's a pity really; it's much quicker."

"Prettier, too," said Patience as they branched off the tarred road into a lane arcaded with huge chestnut trees in full autumnal splendour. "It must be heavenly in the spring."

"It is," said Patience. "You should see the primroses along the river. We always bring Aunt Fan down; she loves them. This is where she was last night, I expect; it's always been a favourite place of hers."

A turning in the lane had brought them into sight of the row of aged willows that marked where the Much ran. Ahead of them, Patience could see a hump-backed wooden bridge in a tangle of trees.

"Hoblong's Bridge," said Gerald. "It's not nearly so overgrown here as on our side, Pen; we ought to do something about it."

But the two girls were silent, gazing at the uniformed policeman who had emerged from under the bridge and was coming heavily towards them. "Sorry sir," he said to Gerald, "I'm afraid you can't come this way right now." He stood four-square in their path.

"Why on earth not?" said Gerald. "It's our own land over there after all."

For all her puzzlement, Patience found herself being amused at his faint air of lord of the manor. But the policeman was far from amused. "Oh," he said, "would you be young Mr Cunningham? I think Inspector Adams wants a word with you. Would you wait here a minute, please? No," he stood firmly in Gerald's way, "right here, if you wouldn't mind, sir." He left them and vanished into the thicket by the bridge.

"How ridiculous," said Gerald. "What on earth can they be up to now? And who's this Inspector Adams, for Pete's sake?"

Penelope had sat down and was examining her heel. "He's in charge of the case," she said. "Andrews told me. Looks as if they didn't think much of bright young thing Crankshaw in Camchester."

"I don't know why not," said Patience. "I thought he was marvellous the way he took hold of things last night."

"Yes," said Gerald, "so marvellous you thought it would be just lovely to go and tell him all about our private affairs." His tone was suddenly so unpleasant that Patience reddened and Penelope looked at him in surprise. But there was no time for comment; the commanding form of Inspector Adams had emerged from the trees and was advancing on them.

"Mr Cunningham?" he said. "I'm Inspector Adams from Camchester. I'm afraid I've some more bad news for you. Miss Hoblong has killed herself."

"Aunt Fan?" Penelope looked up, white-faced, from the side of the road with her shoe still in one hand.

"I'm afraid so. This bridge was a favourite place of hers, I understand?"

"Yes, she loved to come down here," said Gerald. "She used to make willow garlands. Oh—" he broke off.

"Yes, I'm afraid that's just what happened," said Adams. "I'm not much of a Shakespeare scholar myself, but young Crankshaw says there's a bit in one of his plays where the girl drowns herself with a lot of flowers; and I'm afraid that's just what happened."

"Oh, poor Aunt Fan," said Penelope. "She was being Ophelia all yesterday."

"Ophelia," said Adams, "that's the name. So this doesn't surprise you too much, miss?"

"Surprise?" Penelope thought about it. "I don't know. Yes," she had put her shoe on and stood up, "it does surprise me. It's not like Aunt Fan. She enjoyed being Ophelia. Couldn't it have been an accident? She would wear those long trailing dresses and go climbing around among the trees; she might easily have slipped. Oh, poor Aunt Fan." She relapsed into silence.

"It doesn't look like an accident. No more than the other poor young lady did, according to Crankshaw. Flowers in her hands, you know, and a wreath in her hair and just drifting on the water, by the look of it. Wonder there was enough to drown her, poor lady, though it did rain uncommon heavy last night. But you'll be wanting to get home. I think it'll be all right for you to go along now – I've sent young Crankshaw on ahead to break it to your mother – quite a way with the ladies, he has." He realised the inappropriateness of the remark and fell into heavy silence as he walked beside them to the bridge. There he parted from them. "Don't take it too much to heart," he said kindly to Penelope "She looked," he searched for a word, "she looked so contented. You'd be amazed."

94

They found Mrs Cunningham with Crankshaw in the study. She was in tears, the first, it occurred to Patience, that she had shed, and were these, perhaps, more of anger than of grief? It was an unkind thought, and she put it aside, but there was no doubt that Crankshaw was looking desperately embarassed and more than reasonably relieved to see them. Of course it was Mrs Cunningham who spoke first.

"Gerald," she said, "here you are at last. You're all I have to rely on now, you must convince Mr Crankshaw that I am not a woman who lets her imagination run away with her. Explain to him, Gerald, that I know what I am talking about." She spoke as if Crankshaw were a refractory committee, then drooped suddenly on to Gerald's shoulder. "You're all I have now," she repeated, "you must stand up for me." A few more tears fell gracefully into her handkerchief.

There was no doubt about it, thought Patience, she was thoroughly enjoying herself. But what on earth was it all about? She and Penelope exchanged puzzled glances as Gerald awkwardly supported his mother.

Crankshaw cleared his throat. "Mrs Cunningham," he said, "will not believe that Miss Hoblong's death was . . ." he paused, "that she killed herself."

"Of course she didn't," said Mrs Cunningham. "If she was going to do that, why not in the first place and save all the trouble? Why wait till now?"

It was curiously brutal, thought Patience, but there was something in it.

"But your husband's death," began Crankshaw, grateful for the example of ruthlessness.

"Rubbish," she interrupted him. "We hadn't told Fan a thing about it. We never told her things; not if we could help it. It saved trouble."

"But the atmosphere of the house . . . she must have felt it, and being – well, in an upset state already – surely, you can imagine," he paused, hoping for support, but got none.

"I can imagine nothing of the kind. If you ask me, Fan enjoyed being crazy and a burden to us all. Just because she couldn't have her own way twenty years ago . . . and a good thing is what I say – the way things have worked out. It's quite bad enough as it is. Now, young man," she had drawn away from Gerald and stood alone, a rather magnificent, blousy figure in a black satin housecoat, "I've told you what's happened and why, and it's up to you to do something about it. Don't try and spare my feelings. I realise what I've got to be dragged through; I suppose it's the price I've got to pay." She looked for sympathy this time to Penelope and Patience, and got it, though with a considerable mixture of puzzlement.

"But Mrs Cunningham," Crankshaw was getting desperate. "Have you considered? What evidence have you? It's a very extraordinary accusation." He looked round the room for support.

"Considered, young man? Of course I've considered. I suppose you're afraid because he's a friend of your uncle's, but I tell you justice must be done. My husband's blood is crying out for it – yes and Fan's too." She admitted it rather grudgingly.

Gerald's patience gave out. "Mother, what is this all about?"

"Murder," said she, "that's what it's about. Double murder – and for what a reason . . . Oh, how can I tell you, my poor orphaned children?"

"Not quite orphaned yet," put in Gerald, who was beginning to find the atmosphere of melodrama rather overwhelming. "But I wish you'd explain."

"How can I?" she wailed. "Mr Crankshaw, you tell them."

Crankshaw cleared his throat. "Your mother," he spoke to Gerald as man to man, "has the idea that Major Balfour killed Mr Cunningham and Miss Hoblong because," he went bright scarlet, "because he wants to marry her."

"Marry who?" Gerald spoke the bafflement that all three felt.

"Me of course," his mother's figure swelled with tragedy. "Unhappy me."

Penelope gasped, Gerald gulped, but gave Crankshaw the sympathetic look he needed. There was an agonised silence, broken ridiculously by a peal of hearty laughter from the doorway. "Violet," said Major Balfour, "you're magnificent. I didn't know you had it in you. Wasted in private life, I always said so. The Old Vic; that's the place for you. But now, come off it, you're confusing poor Mr Crankshaw."

She looked at him, still with her tragic eyes. "You heard?"

"Of course, I heard. I've been standing in the hall for five minutes splitting my sides. Really, Violet, you're terrific. Perhaps we should get married – after a decent interval of course." The look he gave the children made it pardonable. "It would make it perfect, wouldn't it?"

"But James, I meant it." She was wilting slightly.

"Of course you meant it, bless your heart. That's what makes you so wonderful. Poor Mr Crankshaw's frightened nearly out of his wits. And as for the children – you really should be more considerate, Violet. And, after all, poor old Fan . . . I was always afraid she might do it one day . . . been Ophelia the last few days, hasn't she?"

"Yes, she has," Penelope answered. "But you know," she began "it's a funny thing . . ."

Crankshaw had been getting up his courage. "I wonder," he said to Major Balfour, "purely as a matter of form, of course, and as the question has been raised," he looked apologetically from him to Mrs Cunningham and back, "would you mind telling me where you've been all after-noon?" It came out at last in a rush.

"Mind? My dear fellow, I'd be delighted to. I had lunch here, to begin with – very suspicious, that, I'm afraid. I hope someone saw her after I left." He glanced around the group.

"Oh yes," said Penelope, "Dr Hoblong." It was her turn to go scarlet.

"Good. So I can't have strangled her in her bedroom and dumped her in the river on the way back. That's something. I left about half past two, I think it was . . . felt a bad bout of my malaria coming on and thought I'd better get home to bed. Been there ever since. In fact till my Mrs Despard came up all agog to tell me the news. Ghouls these village women are. Of course I got right up and drove over. Didn't fancy the walk, somehow."

"How do you feel now?" Crankshaw asked sympatheti-cally.

"Not too good as a matter of fact – ought to be back in bed right now – to tell you the truth, this has knocked me back a bit. I don't suppose you know; but I was engaged to Fan once . . . I suppose that's what gave you the idea, Violet . . . polish the lot of them off at once; very tidy. I'm grateful to you, really; cheered me up no end. Haven't heard anything so ridiculous for a long time. Not quite the kind of story one can tell, though." He stopped, shaking slightly. It was true, Patience thought, he did look ill.

"We'll get you back to bed just as fast as possible," said Crankshaw, "but for your own sake, I expect you'd like this cleared up. There are just one or two more questions . . ."

"Of course, of course." The Major sank into a chair by the fire and held out a shaking hand to it.

"Good. Well, first, did you see Miss Hoblong today?"

"No. Not a glimpse. She had her meals upstairs mostly, you know. Poor old Fan." He gazed resolutely into the fire.

"I see. And now about this afternoon: would your house-keeper – Mrs Despard, is it?—have known if you had happened to go out?"

"Good Lord, man, yes. You can't put anything over on Mother Despard. She sent me up to bed with two hot water-bottles, and if I know her she sat with the kitchen door open into the hall all afternoon to see I stayed put. She doesn't like my bouts of malaria. Wasn't best pleased to have me come over here, I can tell you." He looked at his watch.

"And I've been keeping you. I'm sorry. And I think that's about all, as a matter of fact." Crankshaw looked enquiringly at Mrs Cunningham, but she had subsided into tears.

Chapter Five

Crankshaw found Adams and Parkinson in serious conference in Parkinson's tiny office. On the table between them lay the two guns – Mr Cunningham's and the one Parkinson had found in the wood near his body.

"That's quick work," he said. "Are they back from Camchester already? Any fingerprints?"

"Yes and no," said Adams. "Look, you can't have mixed those two guns up at any point, can you?" He spoke almost hopefully.

"Mixed them up? What on earth do you mean? It's impossible. Anyway, we sent the murderer's gun to Camchester before we even knew the other existed."

"That's what Parkinson says." Adams was still full of gloom. "But the devil of it is young Pennyfold identified this as his friend's." He laid a limp hand on the gun Parkinson had removed from Hoblong's Hall that morning.

"He's crazy," said Crankshaw. "Or he's trying to mix us up."

"I don't think he's crazy. I have a nasty feeling he's telling the truth. Just look at those two guns. This one," again the unenthusiastic hand touched the gun from the Hall, "is an ancient battered bit of work with rust and a pawnbroker's mark on it. This," he touched the gun Parkinson had found in the wood, "is a fair age all right, but look how it's been cared for – linseed oil, polish, I

100

don't know what all – well now, you tell me; which is Mr Cunningham's gun?"

"This one of course. I see what you mean. But how on earth did they get switched? Don't the fingerprints help?"

"Help's not just the word I'd use. This one," again he pointed to the murder gun, "looks as if it was last handled in gloves, but they got some fairly good prints from underneath the smudges – Mr Cunningham's all right, after all it's his gun – and on top of his, Miss Hoblong's."

"Miss Hoblong's! Good Lord; you don't mean to say she did it?"

"I don't know what I mean to say. They're playing safe in Camchester; say it looks as if someone handled it in gloves after Miss Hoblong, but on the other hand, it might be that the smudges are from the handkerchief Parkinson used to pick it up with – they can't be dead sure it was gloves – so there you are; Miss Hoblong and some smudges. Personally, I'm inclined to think she did it in one brain storm and did herself in in another. Foolishness to keep a loony around the house, whatever way you look at it. Her prints are all over the other gun, by the way, on top of a lot of other ones we haven't identified yet – Pennyfold's friends', no doubt. But hers are on top all right."

"I suppose there's no doubt about which gun actually shot him?" Crankshaw asked.

"No, that's straight enough. It was the one Parkinson found – his own, by the look of it, poor man. That's what makes me think Miss Hoblong did it. What would these young ruffians want to switch the guns like that for? The last thing they'd want to do is draw attention to their poaching. Besides, her prints are on top."

"Except for the smudges," put in Crankshaw.

"That's right; except for the smudges, blast them. But if you ask me," (Parkinson had left the room for a minute and

101

he seized the opportunity), "our friend Parkinson used gloves instead of a handkerchief and doesn't like to admit it. I don't blame him too much – you can't expect every country bobby to be up in murder techniques – but I don't set much store by those smudges."

Just such superior tolerance, thought Crankshaw, was no doubt being extended to his own all-to-obvious mistakes when his back was turned. But at all costs he must keep his end up in this discussion. "But no poacher's fingerprints on the murder gun?" he asked.

"Nothing but Cunningham's and Miss Hoblong's and the smudges – whatever they're worth."

"Worth a gallows to someone, I should think," said Crankshaw, suddenly sure of himself. "I can't believe Miss Hoblong did it. It doesn't feel right, somehow. Maybe she switched the gun – it looks as if she must have – but couldn't one of the poaching gang have been using Mr Cunningham's gun in gloves?"

"And never noticed it wasn't his own?"

"Might have been one of them who hadn't used the gun before – which would mean he was more likely to have an accident . . ." He was surprised to find himself arguing for Adams' favourite theory that it was nothing but a poaching accident.

Adams looked surprised too. "You and your feelings," he said. "A minute ago you were all for hanging someone; and now you turn right round and want it to be an accident. You don't find the idea of murder and suicide such fun as you thought you would. It does turn your stomach a bit at first, but you'll get used to it."

Crankshaw was furious to feel himself colouring. The shot went nearer the mark than he liked to admit, even to himself. He searched for arguments. "But why would Miss Hoblong kill Mr Cunningham? From everything I've heard up there, the person who needed killing is Mrs Cunningham – he seems to have done all the looking after Miss Hoblong got, while Mrs Cunningham just wrung her hands and complained. There's no motive." He felt that that sounded satisfactorily official.

"Who wants a motive with a loony?" asked Adams. "And she was out that evening, remember, and you yourself said they all acted a bit queer about who was where between half past six and seven. If you ask me they all know perfectly well she did it and are laughing up their sleeve at us – can't blame them for wanting it hushed up, but they must be feeling a bit different about it now she's gone and done herself in."

"But then what about the document and the burglar who broke in – oughtn't that to fit in somewhere?"

"Not a bit of it; the document's just one of Mrs Cunningham's old wives' tales. And I've told you before I'm sure the Smith girl invented her burglar out of whole cloth. She probably did it to put us off the scent. She looks a handful to me; got young Cunningham where she wants him, too. They probably fixed it up between them, with a bit of cuddling on the side. Nothing like hunting burglars in the middle of the night . . ."

Crankshaw restrained himself with an effort. To keep his equanimity he changed the subject. "Mrs Cunningham says Major Balfour killed them both." That should do it.

It did. Adams drew a long breath. "Well," he breathed it out again slowly, "I'd always heard that family were mad as hatters but this beats everything. Why did she say he did it?"

"That's the best of it," Crankshaw sacrificed Mrs Cunningham without a thought. "So he can marry her."

"Old Mrs Cunningham? Well, I'll be damned." But after he had had the best of his laugh out, his official side reasserted itself. "Have you asked him about it?"

"Oh yes. He came in when she was telling me about it – he laughed more than you did. He was in bed all afternoon with his housekeeper on guard at the bottom of the stairs."

"And he was on the train when Cunningham was shot yesterday." Adams liked to show that he had the case at his fingertips.

"That's right. Unless he shot him through the window." They were still between jest and earnest.

"Hardly, with all that bank and shrubbery between. No, I think we can forget about him. Which leaves us with the poachers and Miss Hoblong – and X of course."

"X?"

"Yes, the unknown. You always want to take him into account. You'd be surprised how often a total stranger crops up in these cases . . . or someone you *think* is a total stranger."

"Oh," Crankshaw tried to sound impressed. "It seems to me we've got enough people on our hands already. There's Dr Hoblong, for one. He always seems to be hanging around the place – and why does Miss Cunningham go scarlet when he's mentioned? Not because she likes him, I bet."

Parkinson looked wise, glad of a chance to contribute something to a conversation that had been carried on largely over his head. "Young Pennyfold says," he looked surprised at the loudness of his own voice, and modified it, "that Sheila Andrews told him Dr Hoblong was always round after Miss Penelope, and she'd have none of him. But Mrs Cunningham's set on having her marry him – can't think why, myself. I can't abide the man, and you'll find plenty in the village to say the same. It's always 'can't do this' and 'can't do that' when we want anything on account of the Health Service . . . but he's quick enough up to the Hall when they want him. Yes, and when they don't, too. He got Miss Penelope into no end of a row just the other day, young Jim was telling me." He stopped, abashed at his own eloquence.

"When?" Adams was interested. "What was that about?"

"This document they've lost – leastways they've found it now, I understand – or have they?" He gave it up and went on. "Anyway it seems Miss Penelope thought Peter Everett had taken it – she was right, too, as it turned out," he looked to Crankshaw for confirmation, "so she lit out for the village to phone him from Mrs Hitchcock's."

"Why didn't she call him from the Hall?" asked Crankshaw.

"Didn't you know?" Parkinson was pitying for so much ignorance of local affairs. "Mrs Cunningham won't have Peter Everett in the house – he's after Miss Pen, and he'll have her too, if you ask me, but Mrs Cunningham's dead against it. So who should hear Miss Penelope asking for Peter Everett on Mrs Hitchcock's phone but Dr Hoblong . . . and off like a shot to the Hall to tell her Ma. Not the best way to get on with Miss Pen, I wouldn't have said; but that's his affair. Sheila Andrews told young Jim there was a proper row – he heard a bit of it, to tell you the truth," Parkinson assumed a ponderous frankness. "He was visiting her at the time – stopped a packet from Mr Cunningham himself for being there. Major Balfour and Mr Cunningham never would give that boy a chance. The Major's the worst, though, he's a terrible martingale." His audience was going to Parkinson's head.

Crankshaw suppressed a laugh. "There's not much you don't know about this village, is there?" he said, to cover it.

"No, sir, there isn't and that's the truth. Tell me something's been pinched today, and nine times out of ten I'll have it back for you tomorrow. There aren't many of them here, and they don't go far . . . but this business of Mr Cunningham," he shied from the word murder, "that's something else again, and to tell you the truth, it has me beat. The gun's bad enough," he had taken their discovery on the railway line hard, "but I still hold to it that a little poaching's one thing and murder's another." He got the word out at last. "And another thing, I've been round the village, and every one of Jim's friends here has an alibi, and a good one. You can take it from me, it'll be the boys from Camchester; they don't know the first thing about how to behave in the country. Come blinding out at sixty on their motorbikes and knock down our children – they'd shoot a rabbit across a lane as soon as look at you. Now Jim and his friends would never do that; they're country bred and they know better. And if only those city types would stay where they belong the country would be a happier place to live in, and that's my last word."

"And you know," said Adams to Crankshaw later over hotel pie at the Feathers, "I'm very much inclined to agree with him. It's quite true that no country boy would shoot across a footpath; it's bred in them. I think I'll go into Camchester first thing tomorrow and check up on young Jim's town friends."

"Unless it was intentional." Crankshaw returned to Adam's first point.

"Yes, that's true. And I suppose you noticed about the row young Pennyfold had with Cunningham yesterday. You could see poor old Parkinson was sorry he'd brought that up . . . Cunningham didn't like him hanging around after their Andrews, I understand."

"And he certainly seems to have hung. But could you call that a motive for murder? And besides, would he have shot Cunningham with his own gun? It was the worst way to make it look like an accident."

"Mightn't have had the sense to spot they'd been switched. I think you'd better go up and have a talk with Andrews tomorrow morning. I expect she'll eat out of your hand.

Find out what you can about young Everett, too, and the row about him – lot of rows yesterday, weren't there? I don't mind telling you I've got Everett half in mind for my X. We've got a call out for him now, but there's not a sign of his boat yet. Not that that means anything necessarily; he's often out longer than this, they tell me. The young Cunninghams were looking for him today, you know, over at Small Harbour. Very anxious to see him, they are. You see what you can find out about it all."

"Right," said Crankshaw. "And there's one other thing. Talking about X; how about young Cunningham? Of course it may have been just that he was upset, but I thought he acted a bit oddly when I got there last night."

"Young Cunningham? His own father?" Crankshaw was pleased to notice that Adams sounded shocked.

"I know it seems unlikely, but he was curiously unwilling to tell me anything about that trip to Camchester he's supposed to have been on when it happened. Wouldn't come across with anything we could really check up on."

"That's true," said Adams thoughtfully. "Three pubs, wasn't it, and didn't stay long in any of them. As if he was preparing for our finding no one had seen him."

"Yes, and a lift back from a stranger. Very conveniently to the end of the road so no one would have seen him dropped. But Lord knows what motive he'd have had."

"Well, he's the heir," said Adams. "It's not pretty, but I have heard something about racing debts. Well, it looks as if I'd better see if I can check up on him in Camchester tomorrow, too. I'm glad you brought it up. Though mind you," he was not going to go too far, "I don't think it's likely."

Crankshaw set off for the Hall next morning with a gloomy if resolute step. All his native snobbery revolted at the idea of questioning servants behind their employers' backs and his one consolation – the unadmitted chance of seeing Patience Smith – had been poisoned for him by Adam's farewell shout of, "Good luck with the girls."

He hated the whole business. Anything would be better than this perpetual asking of embarassing questions, these reckless investigations of dirty linen. He would telephone his uncle. He would resign. After all, he was worse than useless in the case anyway; now Adams had appeared he was nothing more than an errand boy, doing the jobs Adams found too dull. But he had reached the Hall. Humiliatingly and as a last straw, he was on foot this morning; Adams had taken his car.

He rang the door bell savagely and Andrews appeared. He asked, as he had determined to, for Mrs Cunningham, but, as he had expected, she was not up, or at least not visible.

"Oh," he said, "that's too bad. Then, perhaps, might I have a word with you? It's just a question of checking up on some times for Monday night."

"Right you are," Andrews was always ready to talk. "If you don't mind my kitchen."

"Not a bit." He followed her into the kitchen which was still full of comfortable suggestions of breakfast bacon. He liked kitchens and found himself feeling better. And after all the questions were harmless enough. He began, to get her at her ease, by going over the times of Pennyfold's arrival and departure and of her visit to the study. She was positive that Pennyfold had not left till seven. "I was watching the clock," she pointed to a battered alarm on the draining board, "on account of getting my soufflé into the oven. I had enough of a rush as it was. Men are so thoughtless . . ."

But he headed her off what he could see might be an all-too-exhaustive subject. "And what time was it you went into the study?"

"Just before quarter to, sir. Jim got here around half past, and we got talking, and then I thought I'd never asked about those eggs," she paused for a minute, then went on rapidly, "so I went right into the study and asked Miss Pen."

Crankshaw suddenly had a memory of his mother frenziedly beating eggs for a soufflé. "I thought you were out of eggs," he said. "Wasn't that what you went to ask Miss Cunningham about?"

"Yes." She looked uncomfortable and began to polish the glasses on the draining board with unnecessary zeal.

"Then how did you manage to make a soufflé after all? I remember it. It was burnt when I got here." Andrews polished glasses with desperation and said nothing and he went on. "You wanted an excuse to go into the study, was that it?" There was a hint of assent in Andrews' silence. "I thought it was queer you didn't ask Mrs Cunningham about those eggs."

"She wasn't there to be asked." Andrews seized the chance of a diversion.

"Oh? Where was she?"

"I dunno. Outside prowling around somewhere, I suppose. Soaking, her shoes were next morning, almost as bad as Miss Fan's . . . took me half an hour to polish them; some people are so inconsiderate. You'd think they'd wear gum boots if they're going traipsing around in the rain like that . . . and mud, you should have seen Mrs Cunningham's. Walking all over the garden beds by the looks of it."

"You mean Mrs Cunningham and Miss Hoblong were both out at quarter to seven?"

"That's right." She looked rather conscience-stricken now it was out.

"And how did you happen to know they were?" He was not letting her off so easily. "Do you always make a point of knowing where everyone in the house is? What was it young Pennyfold wanted to do that you had to be so sure where everyone was? Come on, you'd better tell me; you're making it look bad for him this way." If he hurried her, she might forget that at least Pennyfold's alibi was established.

But Andrews, never a resolute character, was visibly giving way. "I didn't mean any harm," she said. "It was just a joke. Jim was so tired of Bill Hendon and his carryings on about that gun of his, and he asked – I didn't ought to tell you." She burst into tears, making traditional and ostentatious use of her apron.

"I see," Crankshaw had it. "Jim wanted to borrow Mr Cunningham's gun." He used the gentle verb on purpose.

"That's it," she gulped with relief. "To show Bill Hendon. He'd have put it back next day; honest he would. I told him where it was and he sneaked upstairs while I was in the study . . . and then after all he couldn't find it . . . of course it turned out Miss Hoblong had it in her room all the time; though what she wanted with it, I can't think. I was just as glad, to tell you the truth. It was asking for trouble, the way Mr Cunningham felt about Jim already. But of course he wouldn't see that . . . 'What does it matter what the old thing thinks?' he said, 'we'll be in America before Christmas.' I suppose we won't be able to go now, Mr Crankshaw, if you arrest poor Jim. But he didn't do it, I swear he didn't."

"No." He felt she deserved a little consoling. "I can see that if he was upstairs looking for Mr Cunningham's gun at quarter to seven, he can't have murdered him. And if he didn't find it there's not much harm done, I suppose. What time did Mrs Cunningham and Miss Hoblong get back?"

"I don't know, I'm sure. I was so busy after Jim left, I didn't know what was going on, except of course I heard the telephone ring twice . . . but I didn't even hear what they said." She sounded disappointed.

"I see. Now one other thing. Did you see Peter Everett on

110

Monday night? You know he was in the study just before you went in."

"Yes, sir. But I never saw him. And if you're going to try and put this on him, you're making a great mistake, and so I told him." She stopped short.

"Told him? When?"

Andrews gave a hunted look around, but her spirit was broken. She gave up. "Why, yesterday afternoon. He came round to my back door asking for Miss Pen – didn't like to come to the front on account of Mrs Cunningham – but she'd gone over to Small Harbour looking for him. Too bad, wasn't it, missing each other like that?" For a minute, romance eclipsed murder.

"Didn't you tell him to get in touch with us?"

"No, why should I? Nobody told me you wanted him for anything. I told him he'd best keep away for a bit; Mrs Cunningham's het up enough already without seeing him round the place."

"Did you find out where he'd come from?"

"No, why should I?" Again the maddening response. "It wasn't any of my business. He said he'd call Miss Pen when he got to a phone . . . but he didn't say when that would be, if that's what you're going to ask next."

"And what time was he here?"

"About quarter past three. I remember that, because I thought he might have met them coming across from Lesston, but Miss Pen told me they went round by road." She watched with visible irritation while Crankshaw made a note and burst out, "But if you think Peter Everett had anything to do with it, you're nuts, and that's my last word. If you want someone suspicious; what about old nosy parson Mr Giles? What was he doing in and out of the shrubbery after he was supposed to have gone home from tea on Monday night? Staying all afternoon, too, when nobody wanted him.

111

You go and ask him what he was up to, and leave us alone for a bit."

Crankshaw paused in the hall. If only Miss Smith would appear – there were so many questions he would like to ask her. An upstairs door opened and he looked up hopefully, but it was Mrs Cunningham. His heart sank, but it was too late to pretend he had not seen her. "Good morning." He backed towards the door as he spoke.

"Ah, good morning, Mr Crankshaw. I was hoping to see you." She swept down on him, very much in command of herself, and, he feared, of him. "I wanted to apologise for all the nonsense I talked yesterday. Stupid of me; I'm afraid I must really have been a little hysterical. I hope you didn't take it too seriously." As she spoke she shepherded him into the drawing-room, and the end of the sentence found him settled helplessly in a low chair with her erect and dominating in an old fashioned wingbacked one.

"Oh well," he temporised, "we have to consider all the possibilities, of course . . ."

"Yes, naturally, and that's why I wanted to see you. I've had a terrible night thinking about it all. It's not right, is it, to stand back and allow even the possibility of suspicions like that . . . It's my duty, I keep telling myself it's my duty. But my own sister . . ." She paused, acting uncertainty, Crankshaw felt, to perfection.

"There was something you felt you should tell me about Miss Hoblong?" he prompted.

"I'm afraid so. Of course we should have told you in the first place, but I couldn't believe . . . it's still hard to . . . but she was out when my husband was killed, Mr Crankshaw, and she'd been wandering about with that old gun of his for days. I always told him it wasn't safe to have her here. She should have been in a home; it's the only sensible thing to do with people in her state. But poor Albert was such a

112

sentimentalist. And look what's come of it. Oh, if only I'd been firm."

"You mean," Crankshaw began, but she was in full flood now and swept on.

"She did it, Mr Crankshaw, she did it, and then killed herself. She was always impulsive, my poor Fan." She paused to catch a single tear in a handkerchief Crankshaw half expected to see edged with black. "My poor Fan," she repeated. "I suppose she never really forgave Albert for marrying me."

"I thought she was to have married Major Balfour?" Crankshaw was anxious to get this early history straight.

"Oh, that! That was after Albert proposed to me. Poor Fan; of course she had to do something then, and James was on the rebound too. Desperate, he was when we announced our engagement; I really thought he'd do something violent. I was so relieved when he and Fan fixed it up between them . . . and then of course my father came home and there was the row . . . but you don't want to be bothered with all this ancient history. The case is closed now, anyway, isn't it? You can't arrest poor Fan; she's dead and there's an end to it." She looked at him expectantly, apparently waiting for him to close the case and go.

"Well," he said, loth to disappoint her, "I'm afraid we'll have to tidy things up a bit more. First of all, I understand you were out yourself on Monday night. What time would that be?"

She looked annoyed. "Oh, really, I don't remember. A little bit after my poor husband left . . . I was upstairs lying down before changing and suddenly thought of something I had to ask Fan. When I went to her room she was out, so of course I went to look for her."

"Did you find her?"

"No, it was raining and nearly dark and I came in to get

113

the children to help me and then just as we were going out again she came in."

"Oh. Did you hear the shot?"

"I heard several – there were a lot in succession, quite close together. I remember thinking there must be a lot of rabbits about, for all it was such a wet night. Poor little things, so dreadful shooting them. And in the rain too." She seemed to think it made it worse. "But I mustn't keep you, Mr Crankshaw. I'll tell your uncle how helpful you've been; really it's been a pleasure having you." She was the hostess again, dismissing him. "I don't suppose we'll see you again."

Somehow, before he had time to argue, he found himself at the front door. And after all, he consoled himself as he trudged back to the village through a thickening scotch mist, there was no real reason to see the others.

For once he was actually glad to see Adams' solid form in the comfortable chair in Parkinson's office. He seemed to have acquired such a tangle of facts in the course of his morning that he despaired of straightening them out by himself. Adams' morning, on the other hand, had been simplicity itself. He had found the owner of the gun, who had identified the one found at Hoblong's Hall as his, and provided himself and his Camchester friends with an unshakable alibi. The three of them had been at a darts match on the far side of Camchester from six-thirty till closing time. "And that's the lot that have had anything to do with that gun," he concluded. "So unless we can break Pennyfold's alibi, they're out of it. What did you find out about that?"

Crankshaw told him about the attempt to 'borrow' Mr Cunningham's gun. "And it sounds pretty convincing to me," he said. "Just the kind of semi-illegal mischief young Pennyfold would be up to. And a much more likely way for

114

him to get his own back on Mr Cunningham than murdering him, don't you think?"

"Yes," said Adams, "I'm inclined to agree with you. Well, they're out of it, then, and we're left with someone who knew where they kept the gun and borrowed it – whether he knew that it had been switched with Mr Cunningham's or not doesn't particularly matter that I can see. And so far as we know the only person who knew about it was Miss Hoblong. The more I think about it, the more I think she did it. What did you find out about her?"

"She was out at the time all right." Crankshaw retailed what Mrs Cunningham and Andrews had told him. "Mrs Cunningham's sure she did it. But of course she was sure Major Balfour did it yesterday. And I did wonder today if she wasn't just a shade too anxious to have us close the case and get out of it. Of course, she's an impatient type, but I did wonder . . ." He let the sentence hang for a minute and Adams took it up.

"D'you think she's trying to throw dust in our eyes on account of young Gerald? Not a soul remembers him in any of those three pubs, and they weren't too busy; not on a Monday evening. Of course we'll have to put out a call for the car that picked him up, but the whole trip sounds pretty fishy to me. And there's no doubt about his debts; I've been on to his college and apparently there's been quite a bit of trouble. Betting mostly, but tailors and so on as well; the usual thing. Silly young ass."

Crankshaw suddenly found himself sympathising with Gerald. "But that doesn't mean he murdered his father. Lots of people get into debt at college. I did myself, but I haven't murdered anyone yet, that I've noticed."

Adams smiled. "Ah well," he said, "I expect you're right. I've never been to college myself, nor in debt either, for that matter, so I expect I don't understand. And I'm inclined to

115

agree with you about young Gerald; it doesn't any of it sound serious enough to drive him to do anything desperate. But we'll have to keep after it. I've left enquiries out in case he was seen anywhere in Camchester, but I'm not too hopeful. What else did you get up at the Hall?"

Crankshaw laughed. "Another suspect," he said, "Mr Giles. Andrews has got her money on him because he went to tea on Monday and outstayed his welcome. Oh yes, and she says he was dodging about in the shrubbery after he was supposed to have gone home, which does seem a bit odd in an aged parson, don't you think?"

"Might stand looking into. You'd better go along and see him – he's probably a bird-watcher or something. Treat him gently, for the Lord's sake; we don't want a row with the Church. And how about young Everett?"

Crankshaw felt suddenly like a hopeful pupil being cross-examined on his homework. Still, his report on Everett was obviously worth at least an 'A'. "Over here yesterday, was he?" said Adams, "and never came in to see us. Queer, that. Has it occured to you, Crankshaw, that Miss Hoblong's death might not have been suicide?"

It was a horrid thought that had crept about at the back of Crankshaw's mind, and he found he was glad to have it out in the open. "I've been wondering," he said, "off and on; it seems too pat, somehow, doesn't it? One murder, one suicide, finish. You can't help wondering."

"Yes, and a very neat and tidy way to do two murders, too. And young Everett on the spot both times. We'd better get hold of that young man. I'll put out another call."

"But why would he have done it?"

"Money, of course. Everyone says he was after Miss Cunningham . . . he might have figured that the two of them out of the way meant less opposition and more cash. You would have thought he'd have done in Mrs Cunningham

116

too and made a clean sweep of it while he was at it, but maybe he will; after all it's only two days. Not bad going, really." There was a cheerful callousness about Adams that impressed and appalled Crankshaw.

"Oh, one thing," he remembered something. "Andrews said she didn't know where Everett came from yesterday, but she said something about thinking he'd have met Miss Cunningham and the others on his way . . . which makes it look as if he came from Lesston way, doesn't it?"

"Good work," said Adams. "They were looking for him at Small Harbour, weren't they . . . so he can't have been there. But he might have been over at Great Harbour; it's only two miles further on if you take the footpaths. I think I'll drive over there and see if I don't lay my hands on him. Even if he didn't do it, he might have seen something. And you'd better go and see what the vicar was doing in the shrubbery on Monday evening. Perhaps he saw something. Lord, what I wouldn't give for one real witness instead of all these people dodging about in shrubberies. Oh," he turned back at the door, "you might as well find out what the vicar was doing yesterday afternoon too – between three and five seems to be the time . . . the Doctor was with Miss Hoblong till three."

"And I suppose it was about five when we got there asking for her." Crankshaw did his best to keep the reproach out of his voice. "Was the doctor the last person to see her alive?" he went on rather hurriedly.

"Unless someone's keeping quiet . . . but here we are talking about her death as if it was murder . . . and really I bet you she did for Cunningham and killed herself; I hate to agree with Mrs Cunningham, but there it is. I wish to goodness she'd left a note."

"Very thoughtless of her," said Crankshaw. As he spoke the door opened behind Adams and a head of very curly fair

117

hair appeared around it. "Is this where I come to confess?" The door opened further and a tall young man found himself suddenly face-to-face with Adams. It did not take him aback in the least. "Ah," he looked the uniform up and down, "the great man himself. Parkinson says you're looking for me – Peter Everett at your service." His cheerful face sobered. "It's ghastly about poor Miss Hoblong," he said. "I only just heard. How did it happen?"

But Adams was maintaining his dignity. "And pray why didn't you come to us yesterday – led us a fine dance, you have. Where did Parkinson find you in the end?"

"Find me? In the Three Feathers, of course, hearing all about it. I thought I ought to come to you anyway as soon as I heard about poor Miss Hoblong. I'd never thought she'd do herself in – she seemed to enjoy being crazy, somehow. I heard her talking to someone just yesterday afternoon, gay as a lark and mad as you please . . . it's hard to believe . . ."

"You heard her talking? What time?" Adams tried, and failed, to sound casual.

"Oh, half past three, quarter to four, something like that. I'd been up to the Hall and found Pen wasn't in; I was on my way back. I didn't like to go by the shortcut, somehow – Andrews'd just been telling me about poor Mr Cunningham – did you know Pennyfold's poaching friends keep a gun on the railway line? Oh, I can see you do – don't tell me that was the one. I wondered . . . poor old Pen, what a frightful accident." He was thoroughly serious now.

"Where did you hear Miss Hoblong?" Adams was not to be side-tracked.

"Oh sorry, down by Hoblong's Bridge . . . it sounded as if she was in the meadow right down by the stream – she goes there a lot for primroses in the spring – went, I mean; poor old dear."

"Who was she talking to?"

"I haven't an earthly . . . you can't see a thing there, the trees along the path are too thick; and he didn't say anything."

"He?"

"I dunno; might have been she, I suppose, just as well. I just thought of it as a man somehow."

"What was Miss Hoblong saying?" Crankshaw boldly interjected the question.

"Oh Lord, I don't remember; she's always quoting from plays and things, you know. It was some of that: blank verse, so far as I remember."

"Never mind about that," Adams interrupted him. "It doesn't matter much what poor Miss Hoblong said – we all know she was cracked and it didn't mean anything. If we only knew who she was talking to. You're sure you've no idea?"

"Not the slightest. Sorry. I'm not a great one for eavesdropping – besides, I was in a hurry to get back to the boat."

"I see." Adams left it. "Now, about Monday. I understand you were at the Hall at about half past six talking to Miss Cunningham?"

"That's right." Everett looked mildly surprised.

"And you left soon after the half hour and went back to Lesston across the valley."

"Yes."

"Did you see anyone or hear anything unusual?"

Peter Everett whistled. "That's when it happened, is it? I wondered. Lord, I seem to have been in at the death both times, don't I?" He coloured at the unexpected brutality of his own phrase.

"Yes, you do, Mr Everett." There was something faintly menacing in Adams' tone now. "And that's why we want a very full description of anything you may have seen."

"Well, I didn't see myself shooting poor old Cunningham, if that's what you're thinking of. I couldn't possibly have got there in time, for one thing. He was found down by the railway bridge, wasn't he?"

Adams nodded reluctantly. He was clearly giving away as little as possible.

"Yes. Well, I tell you whom I did see, and that's Cunningham himself . . . to tell you the truth I hung around outside the house for a bit before I went in. There was a cricket club meeting on and I thought he'd be going. No sense asking for trouble and I thought I'd see him safe away before I paid my call." He looked profoundly uncomfortable at having to confess to this small stratagem. "And actually he didn't leave till half past six, and then it was in the other direction – and I headed for the study as soon as he'd gone. But you can see," he appealed to Adams, "that I'd have had to have wings to catch up with him after that. I must have stayed talking for about ten minutes."

"Unless he waited for you," Adams was not to be drawn. "Did you see anyone else?"

"I met the vicar just as I turned in at the gate . . . hurrying along like anything; I suppose he was afraid he'd be late for the meeting – he's treasurer, you know."

"Did you say anything to him?" asked Crankshaw.

"Good evening, of course, but he hardly stopped to answer. He looked in a proper taking; I suppose it doesn't do for the cloth to be late."

"Did you see anyone else?"

"Not a soul. I wish to God I'd met that poacher. I heard them shooting while I was waiting for Cunningham to leave . . . I thought at the time it sounded rather wild; a lot of shots close together, you know."

"How about after you left the Hall?" asked Crankshaw. "Were they still shooting wildly then?"

120

"No, I thought they'd stopped – I only heard one." He went rather white. "Would that be it? Quite soon after I left."

"What time?" asked Adams.

"Let me think. I must have left about twenty to . . . it must have been just about quarter to."

"Have you seen the Cunninghams yet?" asked Crankshaw.

"No, I'm on my way now; I was just having a drink to get my nerve up for Mrs . . ." He smiled. "I hope our stories agree."

"Pretty well, pretty well." Adams was fatherly all of a sudden. "Well, I don't think we need keep you any longer . . . but no more disappearing acts, mind. It's inconvenient. What do your think?" He turned to Crankshaw as the door closed on Everett.

"It sounds all right to me," said Crankshaw. "I think he's right about not having time to get down to the railway bridge . . . If Miss Cunningham hadn't got so steamed up, I don't think I'd ever have thought it was possible. Curious about his hearing Miss Hoblong talking to someone . . . and sounding so cheerful."

"Yes, I wonder . . ."

"So do I. At the outside, it can't have been more than an hour before she died. Did whoever it was tell her something that made her kill herself?"

"Or did they kill her?" Adams finished the sentence. "Either way, they're in this up to the neck . . . there's nothing coincidental about those two deaths, that's certain now, to my mind, and what we've got to do is find someone who could have done them both. You'd better get along over to the vicar's and see what he's got to say for himself – don't forget to ask him about yesterday afternoon – and then I think it's time we sat down and tried to make some sense of all this."

"Or a bit more nonsense."

But Adams was not amused and Crankshaw, making his way to the vicarage, admitted to himself that there was not much cause. It looked more and more as if they had a double murder on their hands, and where were they? If the poor old vicar was the best suspect they had to offer . . . he shook his head and rang the vicarage's feeble doorbell.

Mr Giles looked old and tired and the hand he held out to Crankshaw shook slightly. "Ah," he said, "have you come to resume your interrupted visit? I'm afraid, though, that this is not one of young Pennyfold's days to come to me. He should be over at the doctor's."

"That's all right, we've had a statement from him." Crankshaw was unhappy and therefore at his most business-like. "I came to ask you a few questions, if I may."

"Of course, of course," the vicar's face looked pinched. "What can I tell you?"

"What you were doing in the shrubbery at the Hall just after six on Monday?" Crankshaw brought it out with brutal directness.

The vicar sank into a chair. "I knew it," he said. "It was too good to be true. It wasn't meant that I should get off so lightly. I meant to deceive you," he said to Crankshaw, "but I give it up. It's not my line and it's no use. I must make a clean breast of it."

There was a silence. Crankshaw was desperately, of all things, embarrassed. Surely this mild-mannered clergyman was not going to confess to two murders? Homicidal mania? But Mr Giles was looking at him with amusement. "I feel better already," he said. "True confession is good for the soul. I must remember. You think I'm going to confess to murder, don't you? Well, it's almost as bad as that for a man in my position. I've peculated with the Cricket Club funds."

122

"Peculated?" Crankshaw was at sea.

"Oh, well, we won't quibble about it. Stolen's the usual term, I believe. I'm treasurer, you know. There were forty-nine pounds, five shillings and threepence farthing and I gave them all to young Pennyfold."

"You did what?"

"I gave them to young Pennyfold. I suppose I'd better explain, though it's a breach of confidence; but you'll respect it if you can, I'm sure." Crankshaw nodded. "Well, a little while ago young Pennyfold came to me in great distress and told me he'd got Sheila Andrews in trouble." The vicar blushed slightly for Crankshaw's youth and Crankshaw found himself ridiculously doing the same. The vicar hurried on. "He said he wanted to marry her, but she was desperate to get away from where she was known before it came out – anyway, what it all came down to was that they wanted to go to America and needed fifty pounds towards the passage. Without it – well, they wouldn't get married . . . blackmail in a way I suppose, looking back on it. But, well, I had the cricket money . . . nobody was going to want it till next spring – and I thought why not make Pennyfold a loan out of it? There'd be lots of ways of paying it back before then. You see how easy it is to slip into crime."

Crankshaw nodded, devoutly hoping to dodge the sermon. The vicar smiled. "Don't worry, I'm not going to preach to you. But you can see I'm a warning . . . before I knew it Mr Cunningham was talking about a cricket dinner before Christmas – lots of money in the fund he said, and called a meeting for Monday night. I tried and tried to get hold of him to explain, but he was out all day. I went to tea and hung around, but he never turned up – I gave it up at last and walked down to the village with Gerald. Then I suppose I lost my nerve – I dodged back to the Hall and hung around some more, but I still didn't see him. So finally I had to go

123

and face the meeting – and of course neither he nor Major Balfour turned up, so we called it off, and I was spared – for the time being."

"And what are you going to do now?" asked Crankshaw.

"Oh, it's all right now. My bread has been returned to me – and pretty quick, too. Major Balfour came over yesterday to talk about the dinner – and of course I had to tell him – and he wrote me a cheque, there and then. He said nothing need ever be said about it – but of course I must . . ." Mr Giles sighed. "It's good for one's faith in human nature though. Yes, it's been a very educative experience all round, and if you can just refrain from putting me in prison, it's been well worth it. I'm a better man, I feel it."

Crankshaw smiled. "I don't believe we need put you in jail this time. I take it you were at this meeting by half past six on Monday?"

"Yes – I stayed at the Feathers till about a quarter to seven, just in case they turned up . . . Hoblong rushed away just after the half hour – rather churlish, I thought, but of course he was proved right in the event . . . Poor Mr Cunningham – there won't be any meetings or arranging of meetings where he is." Giles took death professionally in his stride.

"No." Crankshaw did his best to imitate him. "And now I wonder if you could tell me where you were yesterday afternoon between about three and five?"

"Down at the Feathers discussing menus with Mrs Dudgeon. Major Balfour gave me the cheque in the morning and I wanted to make it an extra good dinner – a kind of thank offering, I suppose – I stayed till nearly five and dropped in on old Mumchance on the way home . . . he does enjoy a chance to grumble to me. Good Lord," he stared at Crankshaw, "you're not thinking there was anything out of the way about poor Miss Fan's death are you? I did wonder about it . . . she wasn't the kind that commits suicide, you know . . . Mad or sane, she was a contented person – I've only seen her really unhappy once, and that was a long time ago. It's a terrible business and I mustn't waste any more of your time, unless I can do anything to help. Oh, by the way, Pennyfold was digging my garden all yesterday afternoon, if it's any help to you. I ought to know: he dug up my fuchsia by mistake. He's a rash young man, but he only murders plants, I think."

"Good. And there is one other thing. You say you walked up to the village with Gerald Cunningham on Monday night. Where did you leave him?"

"Gerald?" The vicar looked puzzled. "Does it matter? But of course you have to go about your business in your own mysterious way. Let me think . . . oh, of course, he caught the Camchester bus outside the Feathers. A bit too much Camchester in that young man's life, I'm afraid."

"Did you see him get on the bus?"

"Let me see," the vicar rubbed grey hair awry. "I saw the bus coming and Gerald turn towards it – and then, I'm afraid, I saw my chance to turn back to the Hall when he wasn't looking. No, I can't say that I actually saw him get on the bus, but does that matter?"

"I don't suppose so," said Crankshaw.

That morning, Patience and Penelope quarrelled. It began directly after Crankshaw left. Sitting in the study they had heard him arrive, ask for Mrs Cunningham and then retire to the kitchen with Andrews; they had heard Mrs Cunningham intercept him when he emerged, and finally, they had heard her deliver him to the door. Conversation had flagged the while. Penelope was mending stockings, Patience pretending hard to be reading a book. But it was no use; both knew that both were listening.

Penelope picked up another stocking. "Thank goodness,

he's gone," she said. "I hate the police; snooping and prying and acting as if they were God almighty."

"But, Penelope," Patience was amazed. "It's their job."

"Yes, and a pretty filthy one. You can't imagine any decent person wanting it, can you?"

Patience tried hard to keep her temper. She recognised Penelope's phrases as coming direct from Gerald and felt it would be foolish to quarrel at third hand. But it was no use and battle was well joined when the telephone rang. Penelope answered it and Patience seized the opportunity to escape to her room.

Meanwhile Penelope's temper was not improved by the sound of Dr Hoblong's voice. "Ah, what wonderful luck," he said, "it's you, Penelope. I've been called away urgently, my grandmother's dying; but I must see you before I go. I know you're angry with me, but this is more important than that. You'll never forgive yourself if you don't come; it's for Gerald. I can't stop to talk now, but meet me where your old drive runs out through Hob's Wood in half an hour and I'll explain. And for God's sake don't tell anyone what you're doing. I promise you won't regret it."

Penelope started to object, but he had rung off. She stood for a minute and stared at the telephone. What an extraordinary business. For Gerald's sake. A horrible fear that had crawled at the back of her mind all morning sprang into the open. Gerald had done it and Dr Hoblong had evidence. She shuddered. She must meet him.

No one was around. Gerald had gone out early, Patience had disappeared while she was telephoning, she could hear her mother and Andrews discussing menus in the kitchen. Horrible that one still had to think about food. He had said tell no one, but she debated for a minute whether to tell Patience; perhaps ask her to come too. Then the memory of their quarrel intervened. She knew that she had behaved

126

badly; it would be impossible to go and ask Patience's advice now. Besides, the very reason for the quarrel, her fear about Gerald, put it out of the question. She opened the front door quietly, as only she and Gerald could, and hurried down the drive.

The old drive through Hob's Wood branched off just out of sight of the house and wound through shrubbery and woods until it came out through ancient and mouldering gates on the main Camchester to Cambridge road. Penelope walked slowly, hating her thoughts. Gerald had been different lately, there was no getting away from that; but different enough for . . . ? She left a gap in her thoughts, unable to face the possibility. Instead, she turned resolutely to planning how to deal with Dr Hoblong. How to persuade him not to tell the police whatever damning thing he had discovered? But surely he must have decided not to already or he would have called them, not her. Her thoughts wound round and round and she found herself walking faster. She would be early.

But just before she reached the main road she saw Dr Hoblong's car. He had parked it round the first bend of the drive, where it could not be seen from the main road.

"At last." He opened the door for her. "I was afraid you were never coming. I've risked everything for your sake, Penelope."

"But what is it?" She hesitated, her foot on the running board. "Not Gerald . . . ?" It seemed to say itself.

"Have you seen him this morning?"

"Not since breakfast. Why?"

"I'm afraid they've got him then. I hoped we'd be in time. But I can clear him; if you stand by me. Get in quickly, we must try and get there before they take him into Camchester. Once he's officially charged it won't be nearly so easy."

Hardly knowing what she did, Penelope got in. This was worse, unbelievably worse, than she had feared. And suddenly, because it was so horrible, she looked at it again, and it was nonsense. Not Gerald; he couldn't. But he might be suspected; if she could, anyone could. She shivered at the thought. What was the evidence Dr Hoblong could produce? She turned and asked him, but he shook his head, "Just a minute, this corner's a bit tricky."

They could only see a hundred yards each way on the main road and he paused at the sight of a lorry from the direction of Cambridge and waited until it had passed. Then he revved the engine violently and swung the car out on to the main road and towards Camchester.

"But I thought you said we'd catch him before they took him in?" Penelope expostulated.

"Not a chance of it. I'd forgotten I'd waited for you so long. Straight to headquarters in Camchester's our best bet. Otherwise we'd only miss them on the road. You look all in." There was something of the Hoblong she had always loathed in the sympathetic proprietory sideways glance he gave her. "Have a cigarette?"

"No thanks."

"You'd better, it'll settle your nerves a bit. You don't want to be all to pieces when we get to Camchester." The advice was good, but she hated the fat hand that held the silver cigarette case. "No *thanks*," she said again.

"Oh dear," surprisingly he sighed. "You're making it very difficult for me, Penelope."

"What do you mean?"

"Well, you see." He slowed the car down and took his right hand off the wheel to feel for something in his pocket. Now he stopped altogether. "I don't suppose you realise it, but you're being rather hysterical." His left hand closed suddenly on her wrist. "We must calm you down a bit or they'll never believe us in Camchester."

There was something hypnotic in the smooth, professional

128

voice, and his command, "Now, keep still for a minute, it won't hurt much," had years of habitual obedience to reinforce it. But at the last minute Penelope baulked. A violent wriggle freed her right hand – he had been too sure of success and relaxed his hold – and in another minute she was out of the car and standing panting, beside it.

"Penelope, aren't you being rather ridiculous?" His calm acceptance of her behaviour made her feel that perhaps she was. "Of course," he went on, "you must understand that if you don't come too I shan't feel able to do anything for Gerald. I've wasted too much time as it is. Now then, how about it? Are you going to let your brother hang for some ridiculous female notion or other?"

She hesitated, her hand still on the door, when another voice broke in. "What on earth's all this about Gerald?" said Peter Everett, uncoiling himself from the luggage carrier. "I hope you don't mind my butting in, Pen, but if you're worrying about Gerald he was doing very nicely in the public bar at the Feathers half an hour or so ago."

Penelope stared at Dr Hoblong. "You mean . . ." she hesitated. What did it mean?

Hoblong forced the car into gear. "Very well," he said, "don't come, but don't say I didn't warn you. You'll be sorry when the scandal breaks. I wouldn't be you or any of your family for . . ." Failing to find an appropriate comparison he started the car violently and was gone.

Penelope burst into tears.

"Oh, come now, Pen, don't do that," Peter pleaded. "You didn't want to go, did you?"

"I feel such a fool." She did not trouble to answer his question. "I swallowed the whole business; I was eating out of his hand. You really saw him in the Feathers?"

"Gerald? Of course. You've not been trying to convince yourself he did it, have you? Because it's nonsense." By

129

common consent they had turned and were walking back along the main road.

"Of course it is," she was reassured. "But he has been acting so oddly lately – and he told a lot of lies to that policeman about where he'd been on Monday night. I always know when he's lying."

"Oh well, there are lots of reasons for lying to the police besides murder. And anyway, wasn't he with you when your Aunt Fan was killed?"

"Aunt Fan? You mean she . . ."

"I'm afraid so; I heard her talking to someone down by Hoblong's Bridge yesterday afternoon – I could see when I told the police that they were sure it was the murderer. Horrid, isn't it?"

She shivered. "Yes. And I was driving away with him. Oh, Peter . . ."

He took her hand reassuringly. "Never mind," he said. "Perhaps he isn't the murderer. Perhaps it was just an ordinary honest-to-God abduction. You ought to be flattered. But I'm glad I came along when I did."

"How on earth did you?" It had been puzzling her.

"Well, I was coming up to the Hall to ask your mother for your hand in marriage, when I saw you cutting off down the disused drive as furtive as a carload of gypsies. I'm afraid my natural curiosity was too much for me and I went after you – I called you once, but you didn't hear, so I just kept going. And there I found you *tête à tête* in Hoblong's car. I thought you'd gone mad, to tell you the truth, so I decided I'd better come along and keep an eye on you. I hope you don't mind. It was damned uncomfortable on that luggage carrier of his, if that makes you feel any better about it."

"Better! Oh, Peter, I've never been so glad to see anyone."

130

"Good." He swung her hand in his. "In that case, let's go back and resume my interrupted errand. After all, your mother can't really go on trying to marry you off to Hoblong now he's scooted. How about it? Shall we have a stab at it?"

"Let's."

Chapter Six

Adams listened to Crankshaw's report in gloomy silence. "Well, the vicar's out of it," he said at the end, "and where does that leave us?"

"I wish I knew," said Crankshaw. "Discouraged, frankly. We seem to do nothing but prove who couldn't have done it."

"Well, it's a healthy start. Let's think who is out of it by now, and it'll clear the air a bit. First of all, I think we can take it, it's not a poaching accident. Right?"

"Right," said Crankshaw. "But first, are we talking about one murder or two?"

"Two, and by the same person," said Adams decisively. "I'm not going to have two coincidental murders in two days – it wouldn't be fair."

Crankshaw smiled to himself at this conception of crime. "Well then," he said, "anyone who has an alibi for one of them, is out of it. Right?"

"Right," said Adams. "So that takes care of Miss Cunningham and Miss Smith who were together in the library at the Hall, and Andrews and Pennyfold who were in the kitchen – *if* we believe her, which I'm inclined to."

"Especially as Pennyfold was working in the vicarage garden when Miss Hoblong was killed," put in Crankshaw.

"And the vicar's out of it," said Adams, "if he was at the Feathers till quarter to seven on Monday . . . but the

132

Doctor isn't necessarily – the vicar says he left right after half past, which would have given him just time to get down to the railway line, if he wanted to, and I can't think why he should have. But he hasn't much of an alibi for yesterday afternoon either; says that he left the Hall at about three and went home to fill out Health Service forms. Of course that *could* have taken him all afternoon, but he's no witnesses. But there's no earthly motive that I can see."

"No," said Crankshaw. "I can't think why he'd want to polish off a couple of perfectly good paying patients. Oh, one thing I forgot. It seems Mr Giles didn't actually see young Cunningham get on the bus on Monday night."

Adams whistled. "Is that so? I'm not sure my money isn't on Gerald."

"Do you really think so? Wouldn't he have got himself a better alibi?"

"Not necessarily. When you've been in the business as long as I have you'll know that those loose ones often go down very well. It's when they're too neat they're suspicious."

Crankshaw sighed. "How complicated. But you know I don't quite fancy Gerald just the same. How about his mother, though? By all accounts she'd bullied Cunningham for years; suppose she finally decided to get rid of him? She's just the kind of executive female who's apt to think she's God. And then I suppose poor Miss Hoblong saw something suspicious and was got out of the way too. It'd be easy for Mrs Cunningham to get her down to the river . . . and that would explain her sounding so cheerful when Everett heard her."

"And looking so contented when we found her," said Adams. "Not very nice, is it? But what about motive?"

"She may have wanted to marry someone else – Balfour

133

or Hoblong, I should think. She's mad about the Hoblong name; it might be that."

"Well, that looks like about all our suspects," said Adams. "Of course there's Peter Everett, but he says he couldn't have got down to the railway in time and I'm inclined to believe him – we might time it tomorrow – and Major Balfour was on the train."

"Of course there's your unknown," said Crankshaw, "I'm half beginning to believe in him, but I wish we'd get a glimpse of one of his long black whiskers."

"His what?" Adams looked puzzled, then laughed. "Oh, I get you. No, I don't think we need an unknown. I think you're right, Mrs Cunningham's the girl – more likely than Gerald really – she's done nothing but lie to us from start to finish. All these damn fool ideas about Major Balfour having done it, and then Miss Hoblong . . . just cooked up to put us off the scent. I think perhaps we'd better get up to the Hall and see if she can prove she was lying down yesterday afternoon, the way she says she was, because if not . . ." On this ominous pause they started.

Andrews opened the door for them with a broad grin on her face. "Come in," she said. "You're just in time for the party."

"Party?" said Adams and indeed, thought Crankshaw, it was an odd time for one. But there, on a side table in the hall was a tray bristling with liqueur glasses. Andrews picked it up and ushered them into the drawing-room.

"Some more for your celebration," she said inelegantly, plumping the tray down on the table by Mrs Cunningham.

Mrs Cunningham looked at Adams and Crankshaw with cold dislike. "What a delightful surprise," her tone belied the words. "I'm so glad you don't stand on ceremony with us. Some people might think they should telephone for an

134

appointment. As it is you find us celebrating ... dear Penelope has just got engaged to Mr Everett."

From behind Penelope's chair Peter Everett winked broadly at Crankshaw who had settled gladly into a chair by Patience Smith and was watching with well-concealed amusement as Adams searched for an opening. If this was a bluff by Mrs Cunningham to conceal her guilt, it was the most successful one so far. She raised her glass. "We must drink their health," she said. They drank among murmurs of 'good luck' and 'happiness', the scene so artificial that Crankshaw half expected someone to fall poisoned at his feet. But all that happened was that Adams cleared his throat ominously.

"I'm sorry to spoil the fun," he said, "but I'm afraid we're here on business. There are a few questions I wanted to ask you, Mrs Cunningham."

"Oh dear, more questions. Haven't you asked enough by now? It's really very tiresome to have to go on thinking and thinking about what one did days ago ... and besides, it's all solved isn't it? Oh, but of course I clean forgot to tell you ... the excitement of the engagement and all; I'm afraid it completely slipped my memory. How very thoughtless of me." She spoke as if she had forgotten a minor social formality.

"To tell me what?" Adams was formidable.

"Why, that Dr Hoblong did it, of course. And poor Fan, too. I'm sure it's against the Hippo-whatever-it-is oath for doctors to murder their patients ... and his cousin, too. I don't know what the world's coming to, I really don't."

"You say that Dr Hoblong did it?" In a moment, thought Crankshaw, Adams would burst. "And pray, what evidence have you?"

"Oh, evidence," she was about to brush it aside, then

changed her mind. "Well, I suppose you'd call it evidence . . . it was Patience who noticed it really. Such an observant girl; it just shows that a university education is worth while – you must finish yours before you get married, Penelope dear."

Adams was scarlet in the face. "What did Miss Smith notice?" he asked.

"Why, that a lot of poor Fan's tablets were missing – sleeping pills, you know – we kept them in the hall; it was so convenient for Andrews: one before meals, when she was excited. And Miss Smith says the bottle was almost full before lunch yesterday . . . and only a quarter full last night. So you see it must be Dr Hoblong. And besides who · else had a chance to ask her to meet him – she didn't see anyone all day except Penelope and Andrews and him."

"You didn't see her?" asked Adams.

"Oh no, it upset my nerves far too much. When she was in one of her states, I never went near her. And anyway I was too upset yesterday; I stayed in my room most of the day." She suggested a tear with an elegant gesture.

"And why should Dr Hoblong have killed your husband and Miss Hoblong?" asked Adams wearily. But there was beginning to be a hint of doubt in his voice, Crankshaw noticed, perhaps because it was a doubt that he himself shared. This was an important discovery of Miss Smith's, that was certain.

Mrs Cunningham sighed. "Oh dear, it's such ancient history; I hoped we'd never have to go into it again . . . and of course I don't really know what happened. They spared me as much as they could. I was such a delicate young girl at the time; so sensitive, you know. All I know is that Fan and Dr Hoblong – only his name was still Smith then, of course – were both in Brighton on holiday . . . I know because I had postcards from them both," she said triumphantly. "And they had pictures of the Pavilion, I remember . . . and everyone was in a great state at home – it was just after Father got home from abroad. He didn't speak for a week – and then when Fan got home she was dreadfully ill . . . and she's been the way she is ever since. Well, of course, being my own sister, I never said anything and I wouldn't now, if I could have helped it, but of course when he behaves like this – well, what can you think? And poor Albert, too, who only went to Brighton for my sake . . . he brought her back, and when I saw her I cried all day. But of course I never thought about it being Dr Hoblong then. When I think of what an escape you've had, Penelope, I can hardly bear it. Just think if it hadn't been for me, you might have been married to him now. Still, it's all worked out for the best," she beamed at Peter Everett, who grinned delightedly back at her.

"What year did all this happen?" Adams was all attention now.

"Let me see, how old am I now?" She left the question unanswered, but calculated rapidly. "It must have been 1925 – of course it was, how silly of me; I had my hair long that year, and it was the year before poor dear Albert and I were married." She looked triumphantly at Adams. "And it was the summer, I remember, because I thought how nice for Fan to be at Brighton for the bathing – July, I think."

"Do you know where they were staying?" Adams' voice showed he thought it a forlorn hope.

"Of course I don't know where Dr Hoblong was – why should I? But Fan was at one of the big hotels . . . you know, The Grand, or The Royale or something . . . I really don't remember the name. But does it matter?"

"Of course it matters." Adams rose to his feet. "I'm going there this afternoon to see what really happened in 1925 . . . you'd better stay here and keep an eye on things, Crankshaw.

You might call Camchester and have them put a man on to Hoblong. We don't want to lose him now we're so close."

Mrs Cunningham had been smiling to herself. "I'm afraid you've lost him," she said. "So tiresome for you, but he went off this morning. He told Penelope a cock'n'bull story about his grandmother dying – and high time too: she's been dead for twenty years to my certain knowledge." She smiled a conspiratorial smile at Penelope and Peter, while Adams fumed his way to the door.

"You don't mind if I take your car, do you, Crankshaw?" he turned back.

For once, Crankshaw did not. At last he was being given – and by Adams of all people – his chance for the conversation with Miss Smith that he had felt all along would be so helpful. He finished his liqueur slowly, hoping for an opportunity to get her alone. Impossible somehow, to ask her point blank for an interview as he would anyone else.

Mrs Cunningham fidgeted in her chair, then rose. "Well," she said, "I think I must go and have my rest; you'll excuse me, I'm sure, Mr Crankshaw. It's all been very trying . . . I don't suppose there's anything else we can do for you?" She managed to imply that having solved their case for them, she might be left in peace.

Crankshaw rose. "Nothing at all, thank you, Mrs Cunningham, unless you'd care to tell me what you were really doing in the garden on Monday night."

She went suddenly scarlet as only fishwives should. "You're a very impertinent young man and I don't know what you're talking about." She swept from the room.

At least, Crankshaw thought, the question had got rid of her. He took his courage in his hands. "Miss Smith," he paused as she looked at him enquiringly, while Gerald frankly stared. "I wonder," he managed to go on, "if you'd

138

care to come out for a walk with me. It's a lovely afternoon, and there are one or two things . . ."

"Combining business with pleasure," said Gerald in one of his less pleasant asides.

"I'd love to," said Patience Smith. "I'll just put on a jacket."

She left them and Gerald spoke again. "Not entirely the . . . er . . . Wimsey standard, surely, cross-examining a guest about her hosts' carryings on?"

"No," said Crankshaw, "I suppose it isn't. But it makes it awkward when people won't tell one the truth. You, for instance; it's curious, but we've not found a soul who saw you in Camchester on Monday."

"And why the hell should you have?" said Gerald. "D'you think I'm always so disorderly in pubs the barmaids remember throwing me out? I don't suppose you've found anyone who saw me shooting my father either – oh, shut up, Penelope, I know what I'm doing. I'm sick to death of the whole blasted business. But here's your stool pigeon."

Patience looked at him in silent surprise, then joined Crankshaw at the door. As they left they heard Penelope burst out, "Gerald, what on earth's the matter with you?"

"But you don't really think he did it, do you?" To his delight Patience spoke as if in continuation of a discussion.

"No, not really. I think he's in some young man's mess and too stupid-proud to admit it. We'll find out about it in the end, but it's hard on his family."

"And tiresome for you," said Patience.

They walked on down the drive in silence, Crankshaw divided between bafflement over where to begin and admiration for the fit of her tweeds and the way she moved in them. At the gate they paused.

"You don't want to revisit the scene of the crime, I hope,"

said Patience, "because if you do, we're going in the wrong direction."

"Not a bit," he said. "Let's go the other way. The scene of the crime's no help at all . . . neither of them."

"Oh," she said, "you do think it's two murders, then?"

"Not much doubt about it, I'm afraid. Not after that discovery of yours. Why should Miss Hoblong take an overdose of sleeping pills and then go and drown herself?"

"I can't think," agreed Patience, "but it's all wrong, you know."

"D'you think so too?" he turned to her eagerly. "It's funny; it's not just that it's so difficult – excuse me, I know she's your hostess – to believe a word Mrs Cunningham says, but I can't believe the doctor did it, somehow. Even though he has run away – if he has. I wish one could ever believe Mrs Cunningham."

Patience laughed. "Mr Adams did," she said. "Poor man, he did get angry. Actually," she coloured, "it's rather like telling tales, but I think Dr Hoblong must have had some kind of frightful row with Penelope and Peter Everett this morning. They didn't tell me about it, but something happened all right; it must have for Mrs Cunningham to change her mind about the engagement. And he's just the kind of man to go off because he's made a fool of himself."

"Yes," said Crankshaw, "and Mrs Cunningham took advantage of it for another of her stories. I wonder . . . Could she be shielding Gerald after all?"

But for once Patience missed his thought and he was glad of it. "Another thing," she said, "why on earth would Dr Hoblong use the sleeping pills he gave Miss Hoblong himself – it was bound to call attention to him first thing . . . and surely he must have lots of other stuff at home he could have used."

"Exactly," said Crankshaw. "Unless it was double bluff, of course."

"Or unless he only decided to kill her when he was at the house yesterday afternoon."

"That's an idea . . . but how does that fit in with Mrs Cunningham's story?"

"Oh, it might if Mr Cunningham knew something about what happened in Brighton and was threatening to tell. Dr Hoblong might have killed him, and then had to kill Miss Hoblong because of course she knew about it too . . . oh, bother, then he'd have brought his own pills, wouldn't he?"

"Yes, but it would work if she had discovered something about the murder and let on when he was visiting her. She might even have seen it – she was out wandering round, wasn't she?"

"Yes, she was – and oh, by the way, I think I know why Mrs Cunningham really went out that evening. It seems awful to tell on her, but it's really worse for her, poor thing, having you keep asking questions. I'm afraid I saw her outside the window when we were talking to Peter Everett. She must have heard him come and wanted to know what was going on . . . and of course it's frightful for her to have to admit she was spying on Penelope."

"That's a relief," said Crankshaw. "That lets her out – I really half thought she'd done it for a while, but she's hardly the type to have hared down across the fields and done it – what time did you see her, d'you remember?"

"It must have been about twenty to, I remember the clock said five to but Penelope told me later it was a quarter of an hour fast. You remember, it still was when you got there? It's that kind of clock."

"That takes care of her, then. How about young Everett? Could he have got there in time, do you think?"

141

"I doubt it. Besides, I'm sure he didn't do it – he's not old enough to murder anyone . . . and for goodness sake why should he, anyway?"

"I know," said Crankshaw. "Motive's the trouble all the time – and of course that does bring one back to Hoblong; if something did happen in Brighton."

"But why wait all this time?"

"Perhaps Cunningham had just put two and two together and threatened to expose him."

"Or perhaps Cunningham was blackmailing him," said Patience. "They are hard up, I know." She went scarlet. "Oh dear, I shouldn't have said that. I forgot you're a policeman."

"I'm sorry. I won't pass it on, I promise you."

"But you ought to. It's relevant. How hateful it all is." They walked on in angry and conscience-stricken silence for a few minutes, Crankshaw in terror that Patience would suddenly turn on her heel and leave him.

But she spoke first. "I'm sorry," she said, "that was stupid of me. I was lecturing poor Gerald the other day about how they ought to tell you everything, and of course it applies to me just as much. You won't say I told you, though, will you?"

How like a woman, thought Crankshaw, not without pleasure. "No, of course not," he said. "And now we've settled that; what was it you thought they ought to tell me?"

She laughed. "*Touché*, but fair enough. Well, first of all about their mother being out that evening and what Gerald was really doing in Camchester, but of course you spotted that he was lying about that anyway. But I thought, too, that they ought to tell you all about the document business. I don't think anyone's taken it nearly seriously enough, you know."

"You mean there's our motive? But it was returned, wasn't it?"

"Well, it was if that *was* the document . . . but I don't think it was. Why would Mr Cunningham have been so upset about it, if it was just that letter?"

"Was he very upset?"

"Desperate. I think he'd been up all night looking for it. He looked like death on Monday morning, poor man."

"Was everyone else as upset as he was?"

"No, not really. Pen was in a fuss, of course, because of thinking Peter Everett took it . . . but otherwise I think they all thought poor Mr Cunningham was being a bit ridiculous about it. Oh, of course Mrs Cunningham struck a lot of attitudes, but you know how she is."

"I do indeed." Crankshaw hardly dared stop talking in case the miracle of this easy interchange should stop too. "Well, how about the document," he went on, "help me to get it straight. It had been in the family for twenty years or so, ever since some uncle of Gerald's sent it to him from Africa and said it wasn't to be opened till his twenty-first birthday."

"That's right," she said, "and they say there was the document and a letter explaining about it done up just the same – and sealed with a ring of Gerald's uncle's that he threw into the lake afterwards. So no one could have opened them. They arrived all right, Mr Cunningham said, except he said it was a funny thing, the letter arrived a long time after the document."

"Just as if someone had opened it," said Crankshaw. "Was the ring really so unique?"

"Gerald says it was. There were two originally, you know; poor Miss Hoblong had one, but she lost it out fishing one day."

"She did, did she?" asked Crankshaw. "Who was there, d'you know?"

"Mr and Mrs Cunningham, Miss Hoblong and Dr Hoblong and Major Balfour – but it was way down the river, Mrs Cunningham said, it couldn't possibly have been found."

"So Dr Hoblong was there, was he? That makes you think, doesn't it? Suppose she only thought she dropped it overboard and he picked it up. Where does that get us?"

"I'm blessed if I know. And besides, even if someone had had that ring, so they could open the letter and close it up again, how on earth could they have got hold of it? And even if they had got hold of it, it wouldn't have told them any more about the document than it has us. So what's the use?"

"It might have got them interested enough so they decided to pinch the document when they got the chance," suggested Crankshaw, wondering privately how long he could hope for her to keep up the steady, unseeing four miles an hour they had been walking.

"But then why wait for twenty years to take it?" she asked. "That's what baffles me." She stopped suddenly, staring blindly into the reddening sunset. "There was something that sounded odd," she said at last, "what was it? I remember thinking it was queer . . . something Penelope said her father said. I know, it was when you were trying to find out when the document was last seen. D'you remember? Penelope said her father said he knew it was there on Saturday morning – he'd put it there himself. Why should he say that if it had been there for twenty years?"

"Of course you're right," said Crankshaw. "I thought it was funny to keep something that was supposed to be so valuable in a secret cupboard everyone knew about . . . but what he must really have done was put the letter there and pretended it was the document, while he had the document somewhere else – in a safe deposit box in London, for a bet."

"He'd been to London on the Friday," said Patience.

"That's it then. You know, I wondered about that precious document of theirs. Did you look at it closely?"

"Not really."

"I'm sure you'd have noticed if you had – but the seals had pretty obviously been botched together at some time . . . Mr Cunningham must have done that to keep up the pretence. Because the real document wouldn't ever have been opened."

"Poor man," said Patience. "I suppose when he found it was lost he didn't dare tell Mrs Cunningham it hadn't been there all the time. Gerald said she made a terrific fuss about having it in the house – you wouldn't have thought it to hear her afterwards, would you? But look," she paused, "if the letter was there all the time, and Mr Cunningham put the document there as well on Saturday morning . . ."

"Exactly," he interrupted her, "there should have been two . . . and when Peter Everett got there to do his bit of burglary there was only one – and it was the letter."

"You mean the real document had been taken already?"

"Exactly – and by someone who had a pretty good idea it had just got back that day and didn't want to waste a minute – after all they only had till Tuesday when it was to be opened. And then, don't you see," he was surprised to find he had taken her arm to emphasise the point, "whoever took it killed Cunningham so we would get muddled up between the letter and the document just the way we have."

"I don't see why they waited till Monday," said Patience. "He might have broken down any time."

"Yes, that is odd. Still, we've got it pretty clear . . . if this isn't all moonshine . . . that the murderer was someone Cunningham had trusted enough to tell them about putting the document in a safe place."

"Unless they found out somehow."

"That's true, but they'd still have to be someone pretty close to Cunningham. We're back at the circle of people we know . . . but who? It all sounds like Dr Hoblong; but it doesn't feel right somehow. Look here, let's have some tea." They had covered the five miles to the next village in what must, Patience thought, have been nearly record time, and a tea shop of the best copper-kettle variety showed an encouraging gleam of firelight and brass. "I really ought to be getting back," she said.

"Never mind, so ought I."

She was pleased to find him more capable than she had expected over the problems of china or indian, toast or scones. He was not in the least surprised to see her pour out with competence and ease despite the inevitable dripping of the teapot.

"Look," he said over his first scone, "you notice things. Now, think hard and tell me everything odd you've noticed since you've been at Hoblong's Hall."

She smiled at him with the sudden intimacy of their first meal. "Well," she said, "Mrs Cunningham's pretty queer."

He laughed. "Come on," he said, "you know what I mean."

"Yes," she wrinkled her forehead. "And there were things, too. Let me think. Cigarette ash, and Andrews' soufflé, and a faded flower."

"Perfect," he passed her the jam. "I think I know about Andrews' soufflé, but the others sound just the thing. What was so odd about the cigarette ash?"

"It was in the summer house. That octagonal affair you can see across the lawn from the study. I sheltered from the rain there on Monday morning – but it's not the kind of place you'd sit in for pleasure. And it was full of ash."

"Was it fairly fresh?"

"Yes, I remember noticing what neat, long cylinders of

ash they were; the wind would have blown them every way, but of course it was so fine all weekend."

"Hmm," he said, "long cylinders. Could it have been cigar ash? It stays much more in shape than cigarette ash ever does."

"Goodness," she thought for a minute, "I bet it was. I remember thinking it looked a bit odd at the time; and it smelt frightfully strong. There was lots of it. As if someone had sat there a long time."

"Watching for a chance to get into the house on Saturday afternoon?"

"It does seem like it – it'd be a perfect place . . . you could easily get there from the Lesston path – or just round through the shrubbery. And Peter Everett smokes a pipe."

"Good for you." He passed his cup for more tea. "Besides, I think we know all we need to about him now. No, it was our murderer who sat in that summer house watching for all the family to get off to the show."

"You'd think if it was someone who knew the family so well, they'd have taken a chance some other time."

"Perhaps they'd tried. Who was there in the morning?"

"Only the vicar that I remember . . . oh, goodness, yes, I believe Dr Hoblong had been to see Miss Hoblong first thing, but Mr Cunningham was in the study a lot."

"Yes, I expect they'd have to wait till everyone was out – it was the perfect chance. Who left the house last?"

"Andrews. I remember because she was still changing when Major Balfour arrived and there was some kind of a row about her not hearing him ring . . . she told me about it."

"He got to the house after you'd all left, did he?"

"Yes, Pen and I met him on our way back to change."

"So Andrews must have been just leaving when you got back to change."

"Yes, I remember seeing her cut across the orchard from my window."

"And how long were you changing?"

"Ten or fifteen minutes. We hurried because the show was just starting."

"And when you went back to the show you left the house empty."

"Except for Miss Hoblong. She was odd that day, poor thing, too. And the house wasn't empty for long, come to think of it. We met Dr Hoblong straight away and Pen asked him to go back and have a look at her aunt. Oh—" She stopped short.

"It does all come back to Dr Hoblong, doesn't it?" he said. "And if he did steal it then, and she came down and caught him at it – there'd be the motive for her murder."

"You mean Mrs Cunningham was right, but for all the wrong reasons?"

"It almost seems that way – it looks as if he found out about the document somehow and knew it would make the Cunninghams rich."

"And tried to marry Penelope to cash in on it that way."

"Exactly; and when that failed, tried something tougher. But in that case, who sat in the summer house?"

Oh, Lord, I'd forgotten all about that – perhaps it hadn't anything to do with it at all."

"Perhaps not. And what about your other oddities. What were they? Andrews' soufflé and a faded flower? Well, we know about the soufflé; it was just Andrews' excuse to see the coast was clear for her boyfriend, but what's this faded flower?"

"It was a red rose, but quite wilted, and I saw it on Miss Hoblong's lunch tray when Andrews took it up."

"What day was that?"

"The day she died; that's why I thought about it afterwards

– I mean, why a wilted rose? There were lots of fresh ones in the garden."

"Did Andrews say anything about it?"

"Yes, she looked kind of surprised when she picked the tray up and said something about bouquets . . . you know the kind of thing she'd say. It didn't sound as if she'd put it there."

"Where'd the tray been?"

"In the front hall on that table by the stairs – Andrews left it there while she served the sherry. Poor Miss Hoblong; I don't think she ever got her food very hot."

During this interchange he had managed to summon and pay the waitress and tip her so exactly the right amount that her gratitude was unmixed with scorn. "It's all very baffling," he said rising, "and I think perhaps we really had better be getting back. I can't see why anything else should happen but I'd be just as glad to know everyone's safe home before it gets dark."

"Pen's all right," said Patience without malice, "she's got a protector now."

"Yes." The walk back was a silent one. Glancing at her companion from time to time Patience could see that he was deep in thought and, unusual woman, respected it.

Chapter Seven

It was nearly half past six when they turned up the Hall drive and Patience was surprised to see no lights in the study or drawing-room windows. "It looks as if everyone's out," she said, with a quick glance at Crankshaw.

"Yes," he looked worried. "Celebrating the engagement, I expect."

She paused for a minute with her hand on the doorknob. "Have you solved it?"

If there was a trace of mockery in her voice, he ignored it. "Not quite," he said, "it all hangs together – almost – but I can't fit it to anyone. I wish you'd think of another oddity; they've been a terrific help so far."

"I'll see what I can do." She pushed the door open and as she did so Mrs Cunningham appeared at the top of the stairs.

"Is that you, Penelope? Oh, it's Patience – and Mr Crankshaw." She did not sound enthusiastic. "Well, I'm glad someone's come home to keep a poor widow company . . . I must say I think it's very inconsiderate of Penelope rushing off to see Mrs Everett and leaving me all alone. And how do I know she's safe with Peter Everett? For all I know, he may be murdering her this very minute and dumping her body from that boat of his."

She paused for breath and Crankshaw inserted a question. "Where's Gerald?"

"My son," she looked faintly irritated at his use of the christian name, "is out on business. And I think it would be more suitable if you worried about my daughter, who may be in danger of her life this very minute."

"I don't think she'll come to any harm with Peter Everett to look after her," said Crankshaw soothingly "but I'm afraid I must ask what your son's business is."

She looked down at him from the stairs. "You must, must you? And what makes you think that I must answer? I'm tired of your interfering and poking around, young man, and not getting very far with it either, so far as I can see. It's just as well for you Gerald has decided to give you a hand – I wouldn't be a bit surprised if he was out catching your criminal for you this very minute."

"What?"

"I suppose you were too busy to notice the shots a while ago?" She pointed her remark by a quick glance at Patience. "You'll look rather silly when Gerald and the Major round the criminal up for you."

"Major Balfour?"

"Yes, Gerald's over there now. We heard the shots and I made him call James and tell him about it and about Adams going off to Brighton. Poor man, it's too bad; lying in bed there sick, with all this excitement going on, and nobody sympathising with him properly or telling him anything, except me. What are you doing?"

Crankshaw had moved across the hall to the telephone. "Making sure Gerald's there." He dialled. "I suppose you also made Gerald tell Major Balfour I was out?" He spoke across the mouthpiece.

"Among other things." She looked coy at what was obviously a reference to Penelope's engagement. "And James told Gerald he had an idea who the murderer was and asked him to go over and talk it over with him."

151

"What time did Gerald leave?"

"Oh, about half an hour ago – he ought to be there by now. And a good thing too. Poor James, all alone in bed; I expect all he wanted was a bit of company. Really, I wonder he didn't ask me, but of course he's far too considerate to expect me to walk across at this hour of the night."

But Crankshaw was not listening. "Hullo," he said, "is that Major Balfour's? May I speak to him please . . . Yes, I know, but this is urgent. Tell him it's Mr Crankshaw." He waited, his face queerly drawn, his eyes avoiding the others. Then the hand that held the receiver tightened. "In the bath? . . . You can't make him hear?" The replies sounded staccato over the telephone. "Is Mr Gerald Cunningham there? . . . No, no message . . . Don't bother Major Balfour about it. Thank you." He put down the receiver. "Patience," it was the first time he had used her name, "would you call Parkinson and ask him to meet me at the railway bridge, as quickly as possible; and tell him to go carefully. I'm afraid we may be in for some more trouble. I'm going across the fields . . . tell him to come by the lane."

Patience followed him to the door. "What is it?" But she could see he had no time to answer. "You can't go alone." He was outside and took no notice. She turned back to Mrs Cunningham. "Would you phone Parkinson?"

"Of course," Mrs Cunningham was already at the telephone. "I don't know what he was thinking of asking you when I was here . . . And I can't think what all the excitement's about. Has someone murdered poor James now?" But the front door had closed on Patience.

She caught Crankshaw up at the bottom of the lawn, where he had paused for a moment, uncertain where the field path started. "This way," she said.

"You can't come. It's not safe."

"Of course I can. You'll never find your way alone." The

152

dusk had begun to close in while they were in the house, and the valley was heavy with evening mist.

"Please go back. I don't know what we mayn't be getting into." They had started across the field.

"It's no use; I'm not going. I'll take care of myself, I promise. I always do. But what is it?"

"Trouble, I'm afraid. Unless I'm all wrong. Lord, what an idiot I'll look . . . but I can't be; it all fits."

"Fits how?" She spoke in a gasp as the pace began to tell.

"Not now," he said. "Better go quietly." He had accepted her company as inevitable, but kept a little ahead of her.

At the edge of the field he paused, whispered, "Can you hear anything? Voices?"

She listened. "Not a thing."

He hurried on and she followed him until they stood in the lane close to where Mr Cunningham's body had been found. It was Monday's nightmare all over again; but there was nothing there.

Crankshaw looked up and down the lane. It was darker in the valley and the bushes made deceptive shadows; nothing moved but a barn owl in a great sweep ahead of them.

"Gerald – Mr Cunningham," Crankshaw called, and Patience jumped at the sound of his voice.

But there was no answer.

"What d'you think's happened?" Patience found her voice was shaking.

"If only I knew." Crankshaw's was desperate. "I must think. It's no use rushing about looking for him; he may be anywhere. Or perhaps I'm crazy . . . perhaps he was just late. But then, where's Major Balfour? It all adds up; that was the last oddity I wanted."

"What was?"

"Major Balfour's asking Gerald over to discuss how to

153

catch the criminal. Why on earth should he? And it does fit." He sounded as if he was trying desperately to convince himself.

"You mean Major Balfour?" Patience was horrified.

"Yes, I'm afraid so. And I'm horribly afraid . . ." he hesitated at finishing the sentence.

"For Gerald?"

"Yes. Suppose he did want to do something to him?" Ridiculous euphemism, he thought furiously to himself. "It's the perfect chance. Gerald himself had told him that Adams and I were out of the way – he jumps at it and repeats Monday's arrangements. Gerald to walk over and see him . . . but then, what happened? He hadn't much time if he wanted to be back before that housekeeper of his brought him his supper – she wanted me to wait and speak to him then – seven, she said he had it. So he must have come out and met Gerald about here . . . and then . . . what? There hasn't been a shot, has there?"

"Not since we left the Hall . . . I thought I heard some earlier; when we were walking through the village, but I wasn't sure. It might have been a motorbike."

"Yes, I remember." Inwardly, he cursed himself for having refused to notice them at the time, determined as he was to see Patience back to the Hall. "But he'd never try and get away with another shooting accident," he went on. "Patience, help me to think." They had been ranging up and down the path as they talked, looking here and there among the bushes, but now he stood stock still. "It's no use going on like this," he said. "We've got to work it out. What d'you think he'd have done?"

"He hadn't very long to fix it . . . if it really is Major Balfour." Patience could not help the doubt.

"I know, I may be crazy. But I may not . . . we've got to act as if I wasn't. And you're right, it must have been a spur of the moment thing . . . not a shot, like Monday's . . ." he paused.

"There were an awful lot of those sleeping pills of Miss Hoblong's missing," said Patience. "About half the bottle. He might have used them again."

"Good Lord, yes, he might. It wouldn't have been so easy to get Gerald to take them . . . but he might have . . . and then what? They would not kill, or not for a good while . . . And he couldn't possibly stage a suicide for Gerald . . . it'd be worse than another shooting accident. Some other kind of accident . . ."

Somewhere in the course of the talk Patience had heard a familiar half-noticed sound. Now she looked at her watch. "Goodness," she said, "the seven o'clock's late tonight. It's just whistled for Greatton."

"My God, you've got it," he was off the path and over the fence as he spoke. "Where would he put him?" As they stood at the top of the cutting looking down through the mist at the lines below they could hear the seven o'clock gathering steam out of Greatton. "There's no time," he said. "We'll have to try and stop the train. God, I'll look a fool if I'm wrong, but I've got to chance it."

"I'll stop the train," said Patience. "Give me the torch . . . my raincoat's light. I'll make them come along slowly. You go and look the far side of the tunnel; the driver wouldn't be able to see coming out of the dark. That's where I'd have put him."

He was so angry with himself for having failed to think of this that he had let her take the torch and go off at a steady jog-trot down the line before he thought that Balfour might still be around. He started to call her back; then stopped. If Balfour was anywhere he'd be under the bridge with his victim . . . Patience was safer where she was. As long as the engine driver saw her . . .

He climbed down to the line and started quickly and silently towards the bridge, wishing that his heavy walking stick had a sword usefully concealed inside it. He could hear the train making heavy weather of the slope out of Greatton. Once over that and it had half a mile of downhill to be upon him. He cursed himself for not having reminded Patience about the downhill . . . would they be able to pull up for her?

At the entrance to the tunnel he stopped and listened, peering into the almost total darkness under it. If there was a sound it was swamped in the joyful clamour of the train, which had reached the top of its hill. No use waiting. He wished he had his torch, grasped his stick more firmly still in his hand, and started into the clammy darkness. The arch of night at the other end seemed unexpectedly far away; he stumbled noisily over a stone and gave up all pretence at silence. A cold thought at the back of his mind told him that there was nothing there at all and painted a future of suburban traffic control.

And then right across the line as it emerged into the twilight lay a long bundle: Gerald. Horrified at his own selfishness, Crankshaw thought he had never been so glad to see anyone before. And it was all right, Gerald was breathing; heavily, perhaps, as if he had been drugged, but unmistakably and magnificently breathing.

Jogging breathlessly along the line, Patience wondered how one stopped a train. Was shouting any good? Or could they probably not hear. One flashed the torch, presumably, but did one have to stand in the middle of the line? She rather hoped that could be avoided. It was getting uncomfortably dark for taking liberties with trains.

A rabbit started away into the bushes and she thought, as she jumped, that Major Balfour (could it really be he?)

might have lingered to see his accident accomplish itself. There was a dark shadow in the bushes ahead of her, and she crossed to the other side of the line, mocking herself as she did so. Of course he had hurried back to bed to present a convincing invalid front for the arrival of his supper. She shuddered at the thought and wished that sleepers were not so carefully arranged to break one's stride. She also wished that the train did not sound so near. It was coming faster now and she realised that the track sloped steadily down towards her.

The engine driver and fireman were discussing in sociable shouts the rival merits of tea and guinness for the end of the run. "Tea for mine," said the driver. "God almighty, what's that?"

The passenger (there was only one) was filling out forms with his biro when the train stopped with such a jerk that he hit his head on the opposite wall of the compartment. Leaning angrily out the window, he heard the driver winding up an outburst of language so magnificent that it could have only been occasioned by terror. "And," he concluded, "you might have been killed and serve you right." He used several adjectives, and altogether the speech seemed to have done him good, as he looked quite kindly down at Patience, who stood, white and shaking, by the engine.

"I'm sorry," she said weakly. "I didn't seem to be able to jump clear."

"I know," said the driver, "hypnotises you, they say. But if you didn't want to get killed, what the hell did you do it for?"

"I'm sorry, I should have explained. We think there's a body on the line." It sounded even sillier than she had feared.

"A body? You should know about it. There nearly was,

157

all right. But what makes you think so? Have you seen it?"

"No, but Mr Crankshaw's looking for it."

"Oh, him. My sister's cousin's boy says he's all right . . . Jim Pennyfold, that is," he explained for the fireman's benefit. "What does he want me to do?"

"Go slowly, so he can stop you. We don't know where it is."

"Sounds pretty funny to me, but OK, miss. You'd better hop in. You don't want to stay out here in the dark with no bodies."

Patience looked at the train in some bafflement. It was much too high above the track for hopping in to be a matter of easy accomplishment. "Here," the passenger lent out his window. "I'll give you a hand up."

"Thank you." Patience was disconcerted to see that it was Dr Hoblong, but the train was non-corridor and there was nothing she could do about it.

"It's all right," he smiled a gloomy smile. "I won't murder you. In fact it sounds to me rather as if I'm cleared. Did I hear you say there was a body on the line? Because if there is, I didn't do it. I went in to Camchester after I," he hesitated, "dropped Penelope. The car broke down and I've been there ever since. I can prove it."

"That's nice," said Patience. "Then you weren't running away after all?"

He gave her a quick glance. "Running away? So that's the story is it? Well, I suppose Mrs Cunningham was bound to smell a rat that size. To tell you the truth I did have it in mind. I thought the place was getting a bit hot for me, what with one thing and another. But then – well, the car broke down and I thought I might as well come back and face things. No fun running away by train."

"Good for you," said Patience vaguely. She was hoping

158

she could manage not to faint. Being nearly run over by a train was quite an experience, she began to think, watching the walls of the compartment swim around her.

"I'd put my head between my knees if I was you," said Dr Hoblong. "I won't offer you a pick-me-up out of my bag; you might take it amiss. Hullo, we're stopping again." They bumped their heads at the window and apologised. "Yes, there he is," said Hoblong. "Energetic young man."

Crankshaw was standing talking to the engine driver in a low voice. "Not dead, eh?" the driver sounded disappointed. "Oh, well then, I've got the very man for you." He leaned out of his cabin and shouted back through the gathering darkness. "Are you there, Dr Hoblong?"

"Yes. What's the matter?"

"We've got a body Mr Crankshaw would like you to look at. It hasn't died, it seems." Hoblong jumped down from the train, leaving Patience to follow him with as much dignity as she could muster. The driver looked at her sympathetically. "Feeling pretty queer, aren't you? Well, next time you try and stop a train, do it from the side, see. They won't all stop so quick as I did. I nearly killed your lady-friend," he said in cheerful explanation to Crankshaw.

Hoblong stood up. "Nothing wrong with him but a dose of something soothing. Those pills I gave Fan Hoblong? I'll be more careful how I go prescribing opiates another time . . . We'd better get him into the train; I've got a taxi meeting me at the station. I'll take him home, if you trust me."

"Oh, Lord yes," Crankshaw sounded suddenly exhausted. "Let's get him in."

At the station the driver and the fireman climbed down from the engine, hoping to be in at the death, and were visibly disappointed at hearing Gerald's stertorous snores as he was carried to the waiting car.

159

"You know, it's a funny thing," the driver detained Crankshaw beside the car. "I was just saying to Sam here that where you found him's just the place I heard the noise the other day."

"What noise?" Crankshaw concealed his impatience behind the inevitable question.

"A kind of a bang – like a door slamming, more than anything . . . as a matter of fact we'd a carriage with a broken window at the back of the train – still have, come to that – those perishing school boys – and I thought maybe that had worked loose, but it was closed all right when we got here. I got Sam to take a look."

"Is that so?" Crankshaw was interested now. "What day was that, d'you remember?"

"Let me think. It was after the flower show, that's certain, but not the same day . . . not Sunday, we don't run. That's right; it was Monday . . . the day poor Mr Cunningham was killed. I forgot all about it when I heard about him; never thought about it till you stopped us just there . . . just this side of the tunnel, I heard it."

"Is that a corridor carriage?"

"Yes, one is, one isn't. I dunno why, but that's the way it is . . . and the corridor carriage always to the rear of the train. And the broken window was at the rear of the corridor carriage . . . you can see it from here, but we've got a bit of board in now."

"That wasn't there Monday?"

"No, it only happened Monday morning some time . . . Sam here noticed it before we started back from Camchester on the two o'clock run . . . no time to fix it that day, so we bunged a 'No Admittance' notice on and went ahead . . . And I'd better be getting ahead now, if you'll excuse me, sir, or I'll be getting the bird at Colbridge."

"Look here," Crankshaw said as they settled Gerald in

160

the back of the taxi. "Can you manage him? I've got to do some telephoning right away."

"Yes, of course. He'll be all right. I'll take him straight home." Hoblong looked enquiringly at Patience as Crankshaw, who had apparently forgotten her existence, vanished into the station. "D'you want a lift back? I'll try not to murder you."

"No thanks. I'm not scared, but I think I'll stick around for a bit and see what happens."

"Right you are." The car backed out of the yard and was gone, leaving Patience to wish she had accompanied him. Geoffrey Crankshaw had forgotten she was alive, let alone wanting her around.

But he appeared, looking desperate, out of the station. "Damn it," he said, "has the doctor gone? Parkinson's still out and there doesn't seem to be another taxi for miles . . . it'll take too long to walk . . . Be a dear and go and see if you can stop a car on the main road while I make a couple more calls. Tell them it's urgent police business . . . and pick a powerful one if you can manage." He disappeared into the station again.

Standing in the road, Patience thought wryly that this seemed to be her day for stopping things. Better manage less desperately with the car, though. She let a baby Austen pass as hardly powerful enough for Crankshaw and was in turn passed with haughty gestures by two respectable family cars. She was still swearing at them under her breath when an enormous Rolls Royce swooped down at her. This was the thing. She prayed for its brakes and stepped into the road.

They worked with a scream, and a furious red face looked at her. "Now then, young lady, what d'you think you're playing at? Gangster's moll eh? Don't you know there's a law against that kind of thing?"

161

She managed to interrupt him. "It's police business," she said. "Urgent." Her legs were trembling again.

He glowered at her. "And I suppose you're the chief inspector? What else d'you want me to believe."

"No, really," she was beginning, when she heard Crankshaw's voice. "Nice work," he came up behind Patience. "I hope you don't mind, sir . . . good Lord, Uncle Timothy."

"Hmmph," snorted the red face. "I might have known it was you. Gallivanting round the country with girls while Adams solves the case. He called me up to say he was going to Brighton to fix things . . . seemed to think it might be a good idea if I kept an eye on you. So here I am. What's this about urgent police business?"

"It is urgent. I know who did it. It's Major Balfour and he's just had a try at young Gerald Cunningham – he'll be all right, the doctor says . . . But the trouble is I'm afraid if that housekeeper of his tells him I called up when he was out fixing up young Cunningham he'll know the fat's in the fire. And I bet she does; I told her not to bother, but I'm afraid I must have sounded a bit excited. She's bound to have spotted it. I couldn't order her not to tell him, could I?" He sounded anxious.

"You could have, if you liked, but she'd have told him just the same." Colonel Forrester started the car, having seen Patience safely stowed in the back and motioned Crankshaw to the seat beside him. "We'd better get up to Balfour's house. You're sure of your ground?" He cast a sharp sideways look at his nephew. "You've no warrant, I expect, and it's serious business if we ask him to come along without one."

"Oh yes, I'm sure," said Crankshaw. He explained about the invitation to Gerald, so similar to the one that had led his father to his death, and told how they had found him.

"Quick thinking," the Colonel grunted approvingly. "Those trains aren't much to look at, but it'd have finished him off all right. What've you done with the body now?"

"Dr Hoblong was on the train. He's taken him home; he's just drugged, he said."

"Well, you must be sure of your ground. I thought Hoblong was suspect-in-chief. What made you fix on Balfour?"

"A lot of little things, to start off with. I only got it this afternoon; Miss Smith helped me a lot." Crankshaw felt himself going scarlet, and was relieved to find that they had turned into the drive of Balfour's house.

Mrs Despard, the housekeeper, appeared in response to Crankshaw's urgent knocking. "I'm sorry, sir," she answered his question. "The Major's just gone out. Said he didn't know when he'd be back. He got right up after his bath and packed his bag and got out the car and left . . . Yes, I told him about you calling, sir, just as soon as he came out of the bathroom. He said to tell you he was sorry he hadn't heard me call, and he hadn't time to call you right now. No, he didn't say where he was going, but he just took a little bag. Overnight, it looked like."

"Did he take his passport?" the Colonel had joined Crankshaw at the door.

"I don't know, sir, I'm sure," Mrs Despard was beginning to look flurried. "I don't see why he should for just a night."

"Where did he keep it, d'you know?"

"In his desk in the study, I think, sir, but ought you . . ." She lost her nerve and let them hurry past her into the study. Patience, who had been standing by the car came over and joined her. "Men are always in such a hurry, aren't they?" she said, sympathetically. "But they do want to see Major Balfour awfully badly, and I suppose that's one way of finding out where he's gone."

"Yes, of course, but I don't know what the Major'd say."

"I don't suppose he'd mind; he and Colonel Forrester are old friends, aren't they?" Patience felt a wretch, but Mrs Despard looked satisfactorily soothed. "Haven't you any idea where he might have gone to?" Patience went on. "The Colonel is so anxious to see him. Wasn't it a bit thoughtless of him to go off without telling you?"

"That's just what I said to him," Mrs Despard felt on firm ground at last. "'Suppose the house was to catch on fire,'" I said, "'where would I get in touch with you?' And he just laughed and said 'To hell with the house'. Excuse me, miss, but he did. I've never heard him swear before, but he fair carried on tonight." Mrs Despard was feeling visibly better as she talked, her loyalty as employee forgotten in the overriding one of sex.

"Was he rude about something else, then?" asked Patience.

"Oh dear me, yes, just about some travel folders, too. How was I to know he set such store by them when I tidied them away? Looking all over he was, and cursing and carrying on so I blushed to hear him; and wouldn't tell me what it was all about for a long while . . . and of course when he did I could lay my hand on them directly . . . over there in the hall shelf, I'd put them, along with the maps and guides."

"I don't suppose you noticed what travel folders they were?" Patience made her voice as casual as possible.

"How could I help it, with him raging up and down about how he had to make reservations for someone to Dieppe next week, and how could he do it without the folder," she paused, subject, evidently, to a sudden qualm of conscience.

But Patience was full of admiration. "I think you're wonderful," she said, "when I put things away I can never find them again in a hurry." She glanced at the shelf

164

Mrs Despard had indicated. "He didn't take all the folders, then?"

"No, just the Southern Railway one about Dieppe . . . at least, I think he did. But it's a funny thing; I went to tidy that shelf after he left – in a proper mess it was with him ferreting through for his precious folder – and there's another one missing. Perhaps he took it too, by mistake."

"I expect he did," said Patience. "I don't suppose you've any idea which it was?"

"That I have. I noticed it specially because it was what I always call our local on account of my sister's boy who works there . . . porter to the boat trains, and does very well out of it, too."

The men were coming out of the library. "You mean Harwich?" said Patience.

"That's right, miss, Harwich. Oh, I'm sorry, sir, I'm sure, I don't know what I'm thinking of getting in your way like that."

"That's all right, Mrs Despard. We'll be on our way now. If Major Balfour gets back, ask him to get in touch with me, would you?"

They left her there on the doorstep, puzzling over that if.

"What was that about Harwich?" Crankshaw asked.

"He made a great fuss about wanting a Southern time-table, and took the one for Harwich on the quiet, Mrs Despard says."

"He did, did he?" grunted the Colonel. "And the night boat for the Hook leaves at ten. What d'you make it now, Geoffrey?"

"Eight o'clock. You think he's headed for there?"

"I do. He'll gamble on your fooling around with young Cunningham getting evidence – as you ought to have done, mind you – for an hour or so. It'd just give him the time. If

165

he's had the travel folders it's because he's been thinking about a getaway . . . he'll have his passport, and for all we know an open ticket; not that there's any difficulty getting on those boats out of season like this. Oh, yes, it'd be a good gamble for him."

"And what do we do?" Crankshaw felt a wave of relief as he realised that the decision was safe on his uncle's shoulders.

"Phone through to Harwich to warn them, and go after him, of course. If I can't get old Jezebel through to Harwich in two hours, I'm sorry for myself. He'll have some trouble, though, in that old Standard of his. He can't have had more than half an hour's start on us, at the outside." They were flashing through Lesston as he spoke. "We'll phone from Camchester; they won't take so long. What are you going to do with Miss Smith?" As he spoke he was taking her a mile a minute further from Hoblong's Hall.

Patience spoke up. "Let me come, too. I won't do a thing."

"We can't very well leave her in Camchester," said Crankshaw, "the last bus goes at eight."

"All right then, on your head be it. I wouldn't want to face Violet Cunningham tomorrow morning; but I'm not going to. So long as we've no Mann Act in this country . . ." He persuaded another five miles an hour out of the car. He was, Patience realised, enjoying himself enormously and all the more so for having a silent but cooperative female audience in the back of the car.

Colonel Forrester parked with a lordly sweep in the 'No Parking' space outside the Camchester police station. "Now then," he said, "five minutes grace. Geoffrey, you find something we can eat in the car. Miss Smith, if I were you I'd phone Mrs Cunningham. You'll be glad you did in the morning. I'll get through to Harwich. And five minutes,

166

mind you; anyone who's not back, is left." He disappeared, portly but swift, into the police station.

Crankshaw made a face at Patience. "Orders," he said, "I'm heading for that pub – there's a public phone on the corner."

When Patience got back to the car the Colonel was already there, watch in hand. "Four minutes," he grunted, "good. Where's the policeman?"

"He went into the pub up there." Patience had recognised the description of Crankshaw with some difficulty.

As the Colonel drew up outside the pub, Crankshaw emerged; his arms full of shapeless paper bags, a bottle trying to escape from under one elbow. As he deposited himself and his load on the front seat, the Colonel put down his foot on the accelerator and the car shot forward. "Half past eight," he said. "We ought to make it. I told those fools in Harwich to stop him if we don't get there – but they didn't seem to like it much; they want you there so they can have your blood if anything goes wrong. I don't blame 'em. But they're meeting us with a warrant; that's all taken care of. I hope to God you're right."

"It looks as if I am, the way he's run out on us," said Crankshaw.

"True enough, but there are lots of reasons for scooting. Women, you know, money, lots of things. Maybe he was just getting more publicity than he liked, with this case on. Odd chap, Balfour, can't wonder, really. What put you on to him in the first place?"

"It was Miss Smith, really." Crankshaw leaned back and handed her a limp sausage roll and a paper container full of sherry. "She insisted there must be some connection between the murders and the loss of that family document of theirs, and the more I've thought about it, the more likely it seems. And then it all leads back to Balfour . . . You know about the document, don't you, and how there were two sealed with a family ring that's been destroyed?" He turned to his uncle.

"Oh yes, I've heard about 'em all right." The Colonel wove the car in and out of a procession of slow-moving lorries. "Never thought much about 'em, to tell you the truth; fool of a woman, Mrs Cunningham; can't believe a word she says. I meant to warn you the other day but you rushed off in such a hurry."

"You mean you left me to find out for myself," Crankshaw laughed. "I did all right. But to go back to the documents. Did you know there were originally two rings? Miss Hoblong had one as well as her brother – eldest son and daughter affair – and hers is supposed to have been lost · in the river. Well, suppose it wasn't lost? Suppose she'd given it to Major Balfour – she was engaged to him at the time. Then where are your unbreakable seals?"

"But how'd he get hold of the things to break them?" asked the Colonel. "I thought Gerald Hoblong sent them back from Africa or something."

"Yes, he did. But wasn't Balfour abroad too at the time? It was just after his engagement with Miss Hoblong was broken off . . . as I understand it there was a bit of a row about it all and as a result both he and Gerald went off for a bit. Isn't that right?"

"Oh, yes, that's right enough. A fine fuss there was at the time. But they didn't go off together."

"No, I don't suppose they did. But my theory is that Balfour turned up in Gerald's camp in Africa just as he was dying. In his last letter – the one that turned up in place of the document – Gerald said something about 'guess who's turned up' or something of the kind . . . you know, the kind of phrase you use when you're going to speak of someone the person you're writing to knows. And then he never named him . . . and I just wondered if that wasn't

168

perhaps Balfour and for some reason Gerald decided not to mention his name."

"You know," Patience interrupted apologetically from the back of the car, "I was looking at that letter again this morning . . . the last page is only half a sheet and it looks as if it had been cut off with a knife." She subsided, grateful to the sherry for her courage.

"Good Lord," said Crankshaw. "You mean Gerald gave Balfour the letter to take back with him and Balfour opened it and cut off a bit about how he was there and Gerald didn't feel like trusting him with the document . . . because it's clear enough from what there is that Gerald decided at the last moment to switch the letter and the document. But why wouldn't he trust Balfour?"

"I think I can give you a reason for that," said the Colonel. "If I have to; but we won't go into it right now. So by your theory Gerald Hoblong gave the letter to Balfour, he opened it up, decided the document would be worth getting hold of, cut off the reference to himself, sealed it up again with the duplicate ring he'd got off Miss Hoblong, sent it off and came along home to wait for a chance to get the document. I suppose you argue Gerald had dropped some hint, or he'd picked up something in the camp about what the document was?"

"That's it," said Crankshaw and held his breath while his uncle took them through a flock of sheep that had strayed into the road.

"Damned mutton," said the Colonel. "But why didn't he pinch it right away?"

"We thought perhaps Mr Cunningham put the document in a safe deposit box or something in London, without telling anyone, and left the letter with the seals botched up in its place. Mrs Cunningham was pretty set on having it kept in that ridiculous secret cupboard, by what I gather."

"Lord, yes. Silly woman. Poor Cunningham; it's just what he'd have done . . . and might have been fool enough to tell the Major, too. They were good friends, or seemed to be; I suppose that would be the Major's game. So he'd know when Cunningham brought it back from London."

"Yes," said Crankshaw. "The day before the flower show, we think. So Balfour didn't lose much time."

"How did he do it? That house is always so damned full of Mrs Cunningham there isn't a chance to get away yourself, let alone take anything."

"We think he waited in that old summer house in the garden till he saw them all go to the show . . . Miss Smith found it full of ash on the Monday morning – cigar ash by the sound of it."

"That sounds like Balfour all right. Though the doctor smokes them too – when he can get them; he's always broke, poor man. I can't think why; it's a fair practice."

"Yes, but he was at the show early helping arrange things . . . and Miss Smith and Miss Cunningham met the Major coming over from the Hall very late and very breathless just before the show began . . . He'd been there all alone except for the maid, who was up changing. It was the perfect chance."

"And what about young Everett?"

"He came along later, after the Major had taken the real document, and pinched the letter and hid it to pay Mrs Cunningham back. Because of course when Balfour got there, there must have been two of them there: the document and the letter got up to look like it, but he'd know which one to take. Poor Cunningham must have been in a terrible spot when he found they'd both been pinched; not wanting to say the two of them had been there in case his wife started asking embarassing questions about where the document had been all the time."

170

"Oh, goodness," Patience had finished her second mug of sherry. "That's why he kept putting us off when we asked about the letter. He was afraid it would all come out."

"And the Major killed him before he decided to face it, and hoped no one would ever work out quite what had happened. Of course, having Everett take the letter was just sheer luck for him."

"That's all very well," said the Colonel, "but what about that alibi of his? He was on the train when Cunningham was killed. You're not going to tell me he took a pot-shot at him from the window and then threw the gun clear across to him, are you?"

"No, it's not as bad as that. It was ingenious though, if you like. As I see it, he went into Camchester on the eleven fifty that morning, sat in the back compartment of the train and broke the window. When he got to Camchester he reported it, high and mighty, to the station master – boys fooling around again; you can imagine the kind of thing, and went on to London as he'd said he would. His ticket was given up in London all right; we checked on that. Then, I think, he came back on the three o'clock stopping train and got out somewhere up the line and came back by bus . . . he'd have plenty of time and there's not much chance of being noticed on those long distance buses on the coast road from Camchester . . . he probably disguised himself a bit and got off a mile or so away from the Lesston turn and walked it . . . and got to the valley in time to catch Cunningham as he walked across to meet him. Cunningham was always punctual; he could rely on him."

"Yes," said Patience, "he said that very thing himself when he was arranging to meet Cunningham."

"Just to put him on his metal, no doubt. So Cunningham turns up just before quarter to, planning to be up at Balfour's place by seven; Balfour shoots him with the gun he's picked up from the hut on the line, drops it near the body – it'll incriminate the poachers, not him – and hurries down to the embankment. It was pretty dark that evening, remember, and I think he waited for the train just the far side of the tunnel, caught the broken window of the last carriage, swung himself up – the train's going very slowly up hill there – opened the door and was in before anyone had a chance to notice. That carriage is a corridor, so he could move down so as not to draw attention to himself by getting out of the compartment with the broken window and the 'No Admission' sign."

"Very ingenious," said the Colonel. "But how do you propose to prove it?"

"There are a couple of points. He left young Gerald's body at the same place tonight – I suppose he was in too much of a hurry to work out a whole new plan – and that reminded the engine driver that he'd heard a noise just there on Monday night – it sounded like a carriage door banging, he said; but they were all fastened when he got to Muchton. And we can't find anyone at Camchester who saw Balfour get into the train there. Of course that's no proof, but it's interesting."

"Yes," said the Colonel, "there's usually someone hanging around there noticing things. Pass me something to eat, Geoffrey, this is the only straight stretch of road; we've got five minutes in hand, as I reckon it." He slowed to a conservative fifty and took a bite of sausage roll.

"Shall I drive for a bit?"

"Not likely. I'll wreck her myself if she's got to be wrecked. You explain to me how Balfour got Miss Hoblong out to the bridge and murdered her without ever going near her to arrange it and without leaving home all afternoon. And then tell me why in the name of goodness he wanted to."

"That part of it's easy enough, I think. She knew he'd

172

got the ring and he never knew when she mightn't have a clear spell and mention it . . . I think, too, it was from her he'd found out about the gun in the hut on the line. Young Pennyfold told us she saw him with it, and she might well have told Balfour. And another thing, young Pennyfold saw her dodging about in the shrubbery the night Cunningham was killed. Chances are he told his mother that and she's Balfour's Mrs Despard's sister, so what chance is there he didn't hear? Putting it all together he might well think Miss Hoblong was better out of the way."

"Yes, that's fair enough. But how did he manage it? He didn't see her that day, did he? How on earth did he get her to come down to Hoblong's Bridge to meet him; if that's what happened. You don't mean to tell me it was just luck she turned up, do you?"

"No, I don't think so. But I'm afraid my explanation of that is mainly guesswork right now . . . I hope I'll be able to confirm it, though. My idea is that years ago when Balfour and Miss Hoblong were engaged they had some kind of system for sending messages and arranging meetings . . . and what more likely place is there than Hoblong's Bridge? It's private, it's lonely and it's dead between their two houses."

The Colonel gave a doubtful grunt, but Patience spoke up from the back of the car. "And that would explain why poor Miss Hoblong was always hanging around there," she said.

"Exactly," said Crankshaw gratefully. "My idea is that they had a signal which meant 'meet me at the Bridge as soon as possible' or something like that and the Major used it the other day, counting on the old habit."

"That's all very fine," said the Colonel, "but what signal? Did he lean out of his window and wave flags at her, or what?"

173

"No, I think they did it with flowers. You know all that stuff there used to be about the language of the flowers? I think they must have worked out a code of their own. Because Miss Smith noticed a faded rose on Miss Hoblong's lunch tray the day she was killed. She noticed it, she said, because she wondered why anyone should put a faded rose on the tray when there were plenty of fresh ones in the garden. And I think the answer is that the Major wanted to use the code but didn't dare draw attention to himself by going out and fetching a rose from the garden. And the flowers in the house were all dead that day."

"So they were," said Patience. "Mrs Cunningham kept wandering round and saying she must do them, and didn't. Poor thing." She had a qualm of conscience. "Goodness, yes, I remember now. I noticed Andrews put the tray down in the front hall to go and let the Major in and the rose wasn't there . . . I saw it afterwards, when she took the tray up. That was when I noticed the pills were missing too."

"You see," Crankshaw said triumphantly to his uncle, "he must have taken a chance while Andrews was announcing him and picked the rose out of a vase and put it on the tray . . . and helped himself to the pills at the same time, very likely. It wouldn't take a minute."

"Then how did he get out of his house to meet her later on? I thought that old dragon of a Mrs Despard said he never came downstairs all afternoon."

"I bet he didn't. He went out the way he did this evening – from the bathroom window and down the drainpipe. There's nothing to it, I looked. He just had to run the bath and lock the door and he'd got his excuse all ready if someone should look in his bedroom. Then all he had to do was go down to Hoblong's Bridge, persuade Miss Hoblong to take enough of her pills to put her to sleep . . . shouldn't have been difficult, she was crazy, and she'd been in love with him

174

– and arrange her suicide. And so back to his bath. Very neat; if he hadn't tried to repeat his success this evening. I wonder how he got Gerald to take the pills."

"Dissolved them in his flask, I expect. He always carried one. I never liked the man; I hope you're right." Colonel Forrester looked at his watch. "Twenty minutes to go. I've got to hurry. Mind if we don't talk?" He dodged the car in and out among a knot of pedestrians loosed from a cinema. They scattered, their faces angry blurs in the headlights, and were gone.

"It looks as if we'll make it." Crankshaw spoke over his shoulder to Patience. "You'd better stay in the car when we get there. We shouldn't be long."

"Must I?" The excitement of the chase was strong in her.

"Yes." Colonel Forrester's monosyllable settled it.

The clerk at the desk was looking at the big clock over the door when Crankshaw and the Colonel arrived. A policeman and a man in plain clothes were conferring anxiously behind him.

"Ah," the plain clothes man came forward to meet them. "Glad to see you, Colonel. But I'm afraid we've a disappointment for you. No Major Balfour's gone aboard. And the passports were all OK. I'm afraid you've had it this time. We made a special check, but they'd none of them been monkeyed with. And the Captain just rang through to ask why we're holding him up; it's a dirty night and he wants to get started. You've no objection, have you? Your man must have doubled back on you somewhere."

Crankshaw and the Colonel exchanged glances. "Well," said the Colonel, "if he's not there, he's not there, I suppose. There's not a chance he could have slipped aboard somehow, is there?"

"Not a hope. We've had the wharf cordoned off ever since

175

you phoned. And by what you told me he couldn't have been here before."

"No, that's right. It looks as if we followed the wrong hunch." He turned to Crankshaw. "What do you say?"

"Could I just have a look at the passenger list before we give up?" Crankshaw spoke to the clerk.

"Of course, if you want to." The clerk looked surprised. "But you won't be long, will you? Captain Myers hates to be kept waiting. They're late now."

"No, of course not." Crankshaw spoke absently as he ran his finger down the columns of names. "Good God." He pointed one out to his uncle.

"Doctor Emanuel Hoblong," read Forrester. "Well, I'll be damned."

Chapter Eight

When Andrews let Crankshaw in to the Hall next morning her face was wreathed in smiles. "I want to thank you, sir," she took his hat, "for clearing it all up so quick. Me and Jim are being married on Monday and we'd be extra glad if you could come – Jim says there wouldn't have been no wedding if it weren't for you."

"Thank you, I'll certainly try." Crankshaw found the whole party grouped around Mrs Cunningham in the drawing-room. If possible, she was in deeper mourning than ever, and her face showed signs of recent tears.

"Oh dear," her greeting of Crankshaw was lachrymose, "how could you do it? I'm sure he never meant any harm, the poor man. And now who am I to turn to? Who's going to help me arrange all these funerals now he's gone?"

"Cheer up, mother," Gerald spoke from the sofa. "You've still got me, thanks to Mr Crankshaw. I'm really very grateful," he held out his hand. "I wouldn't have enjoyed the seven o'clock a bit; two carriages are too many. You mustn't mind Mother. She hasn't got over the shock of being right."

"Of course I was right," wailed Mrs Cunningham. "I always am only nobody ever believes me. And if your poor father had just put that wretched document in a safe deposit box, the way I told him to over and over again, we'd never be in all this trouble now."

Gerald made a face. "That reminds me. Did you find the document? I was so glad to be alive last night, I forgot all about it."

"Oh, yes. He had it with him all right. It was worth stealing, too. I don't altogether blame him once he knew what it was."

"Good Lord," said Gerald, "don't tell me it really is diamond mines. That'll finish poor Mother."

"No, not diamonds." Crankshaw managed to get it in before Mrs Cunningham had finished wringing her hands. "Oil. The document itself's a deed of gift from the Emperor of Abyssinia to your Uncle Gerald and his male heirs for a pretty considerable bit of land up in the mountains there – and attached to it is a surveyor's estimate – I don't know much about it, but it looks pretty promising to me."

"Good Lord," said Gerald again. "But why didn't Uncle Gerald do anything about it? Why leave it kicking around all this time?"

"I don't suppose it was possible to get the stuff out then – I think it could be done now; you'll have to see, of course, but my uncle – Colonel Forrester – seemed to think you were going to be horribly rich."

"How nice," said Gerald, "I won't say I couldn't do with it. Good for Uncle Gerald. But, look here, if the land was deeded or whatever it is to Uncle Gerald and his heirs, what on earth use would the document be to Uncle James . . . he's hardly Uncle Gerald's heir?"

"No," said Crankshaw, "that was the snag from his point of view . . . and that's why he stole Dr Hoblong's passport. I expect he thought that with a good start and you out of the way he'd manage all right in Abyssinia."

"I expect he would have too," said Gerald. "Capable character, Uncle James. I still get shivers up my spine

178

thinking how tidy he left me on that railway line. I'll never complain about those trains being late again."

"I don't blame you," said Crankshaw, "but you should have heard what Major Balfour had to say about it . . . that's what spoiled his whole plan, you know. His idea was to chuck you under the train from beside the tunnel and hope it would pass for an accident . . . He'd some story ready about hearing shots in the valley again and thinking you must have rushed after someone right in front of the train . . . but then it was late and he had to get home in time for Mrs Despard to bring him his supper at seven o'clock and give him his alibi. So he shoved you on the line and hoped for the best."

"Only to get home and find you'd rung up and ruined his alibi anyway, poor man," said Penelope. "I'd like to see his letter to the *Times* complaining about the inefficiency of the Eastern Region."

"It's all very well for you to laugh about it," said Mrs Cunningham unexpectedly, "but it must have been very trying for the poor man. And I'm sure he only wanted the document because he thought it would be safer in his hands . . . and I expect he was right; you're so careless, Gerald. I don't think Dr Hoblong will be nearly such a good step-father for you."

There was an appalled silence and then everyone began to talk at once. Penelope managed to outshriek the others. "What I don't understand is why he hung about here so that weekend . . . it was just asking to be suspected, when we found the thing was gone . . . not that any of us had the sense to, of course."

"Yes, of course it was as it turned out," Crankshaw said. "But, you see, by his original plan the loss was never going to be discovered. His idea was to get hold of the document and make a replica of the packet and put it back in the secret cupboard at the first possible moment, gambling that no one had noticed it was missing. He wasn't sure enough, after all that time, of what the letter he had seen looked like, so he couldn't make his copy ahead of time and exchange it; he had to gamble on getting the copy made and in place as fast as possible. Remember, no one knew what was in the document; you'd all have been convinced that it was just a bad joke of Gerald Hoblong's: the paper he had made up was some elaborate advice to the young in badly rhymed couplets."

"Good Lord," said Gerald. "I would have been pleased. But it's quite true; I was half expecting something like that."

"Oh, yes, it would have worked all right. And then, poor man, he arrived for lunch on Sunday with his copy all ready to be slipped into the secret cupboard – and there was Mr Cunningham shut up in the study with his cold."

"Very trying for him," said Penelope.

"Extremely. And to make it worse he had a bout of his malaria coming on and felt so ill he didn't dare come over that night and try to get the copy back when you were all asleep. So he came first thing on Monday morning and found the fat was in the fire."

"How pleased he must have been when everyone started going after poor Peter," said Penelope.

"Yes. I'm afraid that was what gave him the idea of murdering your father. He thought that with him out of the way no one might ever think that there had been anything else but the letter Peter returned. And besides, Mr Cunningham knew he was the only person he'd told about putting the document in the bank – he'd be likely to be the first person Cunningham suspected once the business of Peter Everett was cleared up. His one idea was to keep Cunningham out of the way till he could kill him. He got him outside on a pretext of needing help starting his car and advised him not to tell Mrs Cunningham about the safe deposit box, and at the same time suggested Peter Everett might be at Small Harbour. That took care of Cunningham for the afternoon, and he already had his plans laid for the night."

"Well, I think it's all very ridiculous," said Mrs Cunningham. "Anyone would think to hear you that I was an unreasonable woman and made fusses about things. And anyway if all that was so, why did he come breaking in and disturb us all in the middle of the night like that?"

"I think he was losing his head a bit," Crankshaw said. "And when he got the chance to unlock one of the windows after Gerald had locked up he decided to take a chance on getting his copy in – he'd be much safer with it there, of course – and in the general confusion over Mr Cunningham's death he hoped its reappearance might be overlooked. But of course Miss Smith heard him, and after that he got desperate."

"Poor Aunt Fan," said Penelope. There was a silence.

Something had been worrying Crankshaw. Patience Smith had a hat on. And moreover she had kept looking at her watch for the last ten minutes, and, most unlike her, shuffled her feet, looked out of the window and had taken no part in the conversation. Now she rose.

"It's frightful, Mrs Cunningham," she said, "but I'm afraid I must be going. They're expecting me back on the one o'clock, and I've only just time to catch the bus."

"But you've only just come," said Mrs Cunningham, "I'm afraid it's all been dreadfully dull for you; Penelope's a terrible hostess, I know."

Patience had been edging her way to the door. Crankshaw gathered up his courage. "Let me drive you into Camchester," he said. "You've hardly time for the bus now. I'm due back at Uncle Timothy's for lunch anyway. I really came to say goodbye, Mrs Cunningham."

"Oh dear," she said. "Everyone's going away. I don't know what we shall do with our poor selves all alone here. But I suppose we shall have to be brave and manage." Still wailing gently to herself, she shepherded Crankshaw and Patience into the hall and from there easily and gracefully into his car. The last glimpse they had of her was of the fine gesture with which she gathered her children – both looking profoundly uncomfortable – into her arms.

Patience sat up very straight and looked at Crankshaw. "I'm so glad you asked me," she said. "I wanted to talk to you."

His heart leapt unreasonably. "How nice. Why?"

"Well, you got away with it with them all right . . . I suppose getting a fortune all of a sudden does make one a bit vague; but there are all kinds of things I want to know."

"Such as?"

"What Inspector Adams found out in Brighton, for one thing, and why Dr Hoblong never reported that he'd lost his passport, and what on earth made Major Balfour think he'd get away with it . . . I mean, after all, there must be lawyers, even in Abyssinia."

Crankshaw sighed. "I was afraid I'd never put it over on you. The others were easy, weren't they? I thought I could rely on Mrs Cunningham to confuse things. Do you think she's really going to marry Dr Hoblong?"

"Lord knows." Patience laughed. "And don't flatter yourself you're going to red herring me that way. I want to know the answers."

"I really oughtn't to tell you." Crankshaw looked worried.

"I don't suppose you should; but you're going to, so you might as well get it over with. I'm very discreet, I promise.

And of course, contrariwise, if you don't tell me; I'll have to set to and find out for myself. What d'you bet I can?"

"All right. You win. Anything's better than having the whole thing stirred up again. But you mustn't say a word to anyone – specially not the Cunninghams."

"No, of course not, if you say so; though I really don't see . . ."

"You will." Crankshaw looked at his watch. "We'll have to hurry if you're going to catch that train of yours. D'you really have to?"

"I'm afraid so. They're expecting me. I believe you're dodging again." She turned round in the car to face him. "Now then. What did Inspector Adams find out in Brighton?"

"That James Balfour and Frances Hoblong were married there in 1925."

"Good Lord. Married!"

"Yes. My uncle had a pretty good idea something like that had happened. Apparently it was hushed up like anything at the time, but Balfour and Miss Hoblong went off just before her father got back from abroad . . . he went straight after them and found them in Brighton – married."

"And separated them just the same?"

"Yes; he didn't have much choice. You see, Balfour was his son."

"Hoblong's?"

"Yes, Miss Hoblong's half brother. You can see why their father went off the deep end. And you can see, too, why Balfour thought he could get away with posing as Gerald Hoblong's heir . . . he had his birth certificate, with old Hoblong down as his father, we found it on him. The christian name had been left blank . . . I suppose it hadn't been decided when he was registered. So with that and Dr Hoblong's passport he'd have been in a pretty strong position, so long as the question of legitimacy never came up."

"Good Lord," said Patience, "you can see he might have felt he was entitled to it. The poor things; how frightful it must have been for them. No wonder poor Aunt Fan was the way she was . . . goodness," it was fitting together gradually in her mind, "think of being able to kill her after that."

"Yes, I'm afraid he isn't a very nice man. For one thing, no one was quite sure even at the time whether he didn't know whose son he was . . . that's why Gerald Hoblong wasn't best pleased to see him when he turned up in Africa."

"Oh, it really was Balfour, was it?"

"It certainly was. He read that letter, knew enough about Gerald's affairs to guess how the land lay, and decided it was worth coming home and living the scandal down, in the hope he'd be able to lay his hands on the fortune – and pretty nearly got away with it."

"Just as well Gerald Hoblong did decide to switch the letter and the document . . . if Balfour had got the document, I don't suppose he'd have ever been heard of again."

"No, though that might have been better for a lot of people, by and large. Mr Cunningham, for one."

"Yes." Patience thought for a minute. "Then all that story of Mrs Cunningham's about Dr Hoblong being in Brighton at the time was just – one of her stories?"

"No, there was more to it than that, I'm afraid. That's the messiest business of all . . . he was there looking after Miss Hoblong. He was a member of the family and just out of medical school and the only person they could think of to turn to. And for his reward, Balfour's been blackmailing him ever since – that's how he got his passport. And of course that's why Hoblong ran away; he had a pretty good idea Balfour must have done it and was afraid for his skin. And afraid it would bring out all the old scandal and ruin him. I'm glad he decided to come back. My uncle seemed to think it might not have to come out after all this time."

"Twenty years," said Patience, "being afraid of it all the time. Poor man. No wonder he wasn't very attractive with all that on his mind."

"Yes, and Balfour taking a percentage of everything he earned."

"Goodness." Patience was silent for a minute. "No, you're right, not a nice man. I'm glad you caught him."

"So'm I. D'you know he even tried to make the poor vicar incriminate himself?"

"How?"

"Well, it's a bit of a story . . . Oh damn, here's the station. Must you really go?"

"I'm afraid so," Patience opened the door at her side and got firmly out. Crankshaw followed reluctantly with her suitcase. The uneasy silence of impending farewell settled on them as they hurried through the station – they only just had time – and found the London train. As Crankshaw got out after putting Patience's suitcase in the rack the guard blew his whistle.

"I'll see you again?" Crankshaw put his hand on the door handle, as if to hold back the train.

Patience smiled down at him from the slowly moving carriage. "Perhaps," she said.